Seven Legends

by Gottfried Keller

Copyright © 11/6/2015
Jefferson Publication

ISBN-13: 978-1519160393

Printed in the United States of America

Table of Contents

INTRODUCTION

Gottfried Keller, the greatest German narrative writer of recent times, was born in a suburb of Zurich on 19th July, 1819. The life of this remarkable man suggests comparisons with novels of development, such as Goethe taught him to write: from the romantic confusion of youthful dilettantism he brought himself, by strict self-discipline, to take his place in everyday social life. Left, together with his mother and sister, in poverty by a hard-working but unsuccessful father, the child dreamed away the first years of his development, and the youth was still a stranger to the world of reality when, with the aid of some friends in his native place, he went as an art-student to Munich. There, after a promising start, he sank into hopeless lethargy, which continued even after his return home. Prudent helpers then took the half painter, half poet, once more in hand, recognizing that his deficiency consisted in imperfect education and knowledge of the world. He went to study at Heidelberg (1848-50), and received an important stimulus from the well-known literary historian Hettner; thence he proceeded to Berlin (1850-55), where Varnhagen von Ense, the admirer of Goethe and husband of the prophetess Rahel, made him welcome. Here the germs of his most important works awoke within him. He had already, at an early age, published poems, which showed the influence of the revolutionary *Tendenzlyrik*; now there appeared the romantic autobiographical novel "Green Henry" (1854-5) which he afterwards recast in very characteristic fashion (1879-80). This was followed in 1856 by the first part of the charming, fantastically instructive tales, "Seldwyla People" (the second part, 1874). In spite of praise from many competent judges, success did not come immediately. Keller once more sat at home a dreamer, although now in intellectual correspondence with the best minds; still, it was a bold resolution when, in 1861, the writer, who had never followed any definite avocation, was chosen by his canton as Staatsschreiber, or Secretary to the Canton, and an important and well remunerated office was entrusted to an untried man. However, he proved a thorough success, and felt the acceptance of the post a deliverance from the occupation of "writing-man" so much despised by the Romantics. He filled this office for seventeen years (till 1878); a period during which his imaginative productivity unavoidably slackened. Then when, with the well merited recognition of the authorities, he had retired into private life, or had begun to prepare for retiral, there appeared, in addition to a noble volume of poems, the collection of stories, "Zurich Tales" (1877), the cycle of stories in novel-form, "The Epigram" (1882), and the novel, "Martin Salander" (1886), which continued the pædagogic purpose of his earlier writings in almost too pronounced a fashion. Meanwhile Keller's reputation had at last been established, a consummation to which the zealous endeavours of writers and critics, such as Fr. Th. Vischer, Berthold Auerbach and Theodor Storm, had contributed in no small degree. His seventieth birthday was celebrated with affectionate interest. But the writer, who lived with his eccentric old sister in deadening domestic loneliness, and whom evenings with good friends in an inn could not compensate for the total lack of comforts, had early turned old and ailing; although any great question always found him armed and at his post. He died 15th July, 1890.

None of Gottfried Keller's works seems better suited to secure him admirers among foreign readers than the charming collection of the "Seven Legends." True, it offers peculiar difficulties to the translator, since it afforded Keller an opportunity, such as he met with nowhere else, of indulging the (for him) convenient fondness for very individual modes of expression. At the same time, these little, highly finished works of art imposed a check on his unbounded passion for fabulizing, and are not so likely to bewilder the foreign reader by sheer overabundance of invention as, say, "Seldwyla People," or even the inexhaustible "Green Henry." Yet even they shew his wealth, and that to an astonishing degree.

In his preface to this little masterpiece of his fiction, Gottfried Keller very justifiably draws attention to "the traces of an older and more profane art of fiction" which are to be found in the old Legends. No doubt their primary purpose was edification; but at the same time psychological interest in the famous saints had to be gratified, and mere human curiosity was eager to hear tales of wonder. Very special interest was devoted to "conversion," that inward process which transforms a dweller in the "world" into a citizen of the heavenly city. The history of the conversion of the apostle St. Paul had already indicated its course, along which, still earlier, among Christ's own parables, that of the Prodigal Son runs. After long-continued contempt of the "priestly lie-gends," Herder brought this religious fiction once more to the light of day; but delight in this popular form of story-telling was his immediate motive for presenting a few of them in a modern shape. The Lutheran preacher Kosegarten, however, when he followed with whole volumes of retold legends, was largely influenced by interest in their matter. Romanticism went into ecstasies over their childish tone and their believing spirit, as it had done over folk-songs and chap-books. Kosegarten's book fell into Keller's hands in 1854, when he was seeking subjects for his collection of stories "The Epigram"; but he allowed his scheme of modern legends to drop for the time being. It was not until 1871, when a publisher asked him for manuscript, that he returned to his happy thought and speedily put it into execution. The little volume appeared in 1872, and had a great success, both with the general public and with the foremost German critics of the day, such as Ferdinand Kürnberger and Wilhelm Scherer.

Even from this sketch of its origin, the fact emerges that the "Kulturkampf" mood of those years had little or nothing to do with this little work, as was readily acknowledged, even by the Liberal Catholics Kürnberger and Scherer. Keller had absolutely no intention of caricaturing the Catholic adoration of saints, like Wilhelm Busch, for example, in his "St. Antony" (1870). On the contrary, when sometimes he turns the faces of the figures of the Church Legends "to another quarter of the heavens than that towards which they looked in their extant forms," this positive confession is the important thing to his mind; for the great Swiss writer has no more intention of denying a pædagogic purpose here than anywhere else in his epic work. Gottfried Keller, like his friends Storm and Heyse, regarded asceticism as a tendency detrimental to the healthy development of humanity. And with this conviction he accordingly devoted himself to the conversion of the converted. Like his Naughty Saint Vitalis, he makes a point of seeking out the most difficult cases, self-sacrificing devotion even unto death: Eugenia who flees from worldly success into the rigorous quiet of the cloister, Vitalis who, in glad self-humiliation, accepts the disgrace of evil repute, are safely piloted by him into the everyday contentment of happy wedlock. For this is the author's meaning, that on this very account they become the more worthy of our honour. Just as he relates how a beautiful ancient statue of the goddess Juno was fitted with a golden nimbus and set up as an image of Mary, so he himself now endeavours to take the nimbus off again, that the pure marble beauty of simple humanity may be restored once more. It cannot be denied that his unflinching adherence to this point of view is not maintained without poking a good deal of fun at piety and asceticism, but it is always good-tempered and likeable. After all, the principal thing is the edifying admonition:

Arise! Arise! Shake free thyself
From dumpish, idle sorrow.

Even the Virgin Mary has become above all things an active, warlike, and resourceful woman, more like Frau Salander in Keller's last novel than the far-off, heavenly Virgin; and one has the feeling that it is not without regret that she refrains from the worldly doings of Beatrix or Bertrade. But highest of all is represented a joyous piety, at once declaring for and surrendering the world, represented, more realistically in "Dorothea's Flower-Basket," and more symbolically in the wonderful "Legend of the Dance," the crown of the collection; for this last tale contains the writer's own confession veiled in the most recondite allegory. As the Muses' singing, so splendid and upbuilding to earlier generations, sounded "dismal, almost defiant and harsh, yet so wistful and mournful," so, in the heaven of the present day as Gottfried Keller built it up for himself, the saints' devout hymn of praise to the laud and honour of the Most Holy Trinity sounds gloomy and melancholy, even defiant. And Keller retorts to it with his own song:

To thee, thou wondrous World,
Thou beauty without end,
I also have my vows of love
Upon this parchment penned.

It is this world which is the source of his joys and sorrows. The Devil is introduced as he is on earth: "A silly devil is the rogue, for he is cheated in the end!" And just because Keller reconquers this world whole and entire, full of strange adventures and transformations, for the earth and human understanding, he revels merrily here, because it is here, in the luxuriant opulence of his imaginings great and small, from that Heavenly concerto of the Muses to the nose-pigtails of the doughty knight. His language plays in a kindly, roguish way with the human blunders of the saintly beings who take a loving and loveable human child for a very "Devil's tit-bit," yet find it offered to themselves as a savoury "pasty." His style ranges from the playful picture of the rococo angel-minstrels to the serious painting of the knight riding up to the church with his eight noble sons; and, despite the difference of his conception of life, his sympathies find something congenial in Dorothea's Christian heroism. For these reasons, Keller in this Legendary, most wisely restricted in number, and grouped in most masterly fashion, has surpassed all those who have ventured on to the same enticing ground since him. Even Anatole France equals him but seldom; for Keller has sought to overcome piety with another piety, with that "world-piety" of which Goethe is our greatest prophet.

RICHARD M. MEYER.
Berlin, 27/1/11.

SEVEN LEGENDS

PREFACE

During his perusal of a number of legends, the author of this little book was pleased to imagine that, in the bulk of the tales which have been handed down to us, not only the art of the churchly fabulist, but also, upon attentive consideration, traces of a more primitive and more profane love of story-telling, or art of fiction, are perceptible.

As the painter is incited by a fragmentary patch of cloud, an outline of a mountain, an etched scrap by some forgotten master, to fill a whole canvas, so the author experienced a desire to reproduce those broken, elusive images; although it must be owned that in the process their faces have often been turned to another quarter of the heavens than that towards which they looked in their extant forms.

The huge mass of material available would have made it possible to spin the book out to very great length; but it could only hope to be granted the modest space which it demands if the innocent pleasantry was kept within very moderate limits.

EUGENIA

The woman shall not wear that which pertaineth unto a man, neither shall a man put on a woman's garment: for all that do so are abomination unto the Lord thy God.

Deut. xxii. 5.

When women renounce their ambition of beauty, grace, and womanly charm in order to distinguish themselves in other directions, it often ends in their disguising themselves in men's clothes and disappearing from the scene.

The desire to ape the man often emerges even in the pious legendary world of early Christianity, and more than one female saint of those days was impelled by the desire to free herself from the common round of home and society.

The refined Roman maiden Eugenia offers an example of this kind, with, it must be owned, the not unusual result, that, reduced to the greatest extremity by her masculine predilections, she was forced after all to summon up the resources of her proper sex in order to save herself.

She was the daughter of a Roman gentleman who resided with his family at Alexandria, a city which swarmed with philosophers and learned men of every description. Accordingly, Eugenia was very carefully educated and instructed, and this was so much to her taste that, as soon as ever she began to grow up, she frequented all schools of philosophers, grammarians and rhetoricians as a student. In those visits she was always attended by a body-guard of two good-looking lads of her own age. They were the sons of two of her father's freedmen, who had been brought up in her company and made to share in all her studies.

Meanwhile she became the fairest maiden that could be found, and her youthful companions, who, strangely enough, were both named Hyacinth, grew likewise to two graceful flowers of youth. Wherever the lovely rose Eugenia appeared, the two Hyacinths were always to be seen rustling along on her right hand and her left, or following gracefully in her train while their mistress maintained a discussion with them as they followed.

Never were there two better bred companions of a blue-stocking; for they were never of a different opinion from Eugenia, and they always kept a shade behind her in learning, so that she was in the right in every instance, and was never uneasy lest she should say something less clever than her companions.

All the bookworms of Alexandria composed elegies and epigrams on this apparition of the Muses, and the good Hyacinths had to inscribe these verses carefully in golden tablets, and carry them after her.

Every season she became more beautiful and more accomplished, and she had even begun to stray in the mysterious labyrinths of Neoplatonic doctrines, when the young proconsul Aquilinus became enamoured of Eugenia and demanded her of her father to wife. But the latter entertained such a respect for his daughter that, despite his authority as a Roman father, he did not venture to make the slightest suggestion to her, but referred the suitor to her own decision, although no son-in-law could have been more welcome to him than Aquilinus.

But Eugenia herself had had her eye upon him secretly for many a long day; for he was the most stately, most illustrious, and most gallant man in Alexandria, and, what was more, had the reputation of a man of intelligence and heart.

Yet she received the enamoured consul in complete calm and dignity, with her parchment rolls about her, and her Hyacinths behind her chair. The one wore an azure-blue, the other a rose-red, robe, and she herself one of dazzling white. A stranger would have been uncertain whether he saw three fair, tender boys, or three fresh, blooming maidens before him.

Before this tribunal the manly Aquilinus now came in the simple toga of his rank. He would much rather have uttered his passion in more intimate and tender fashion; but, when he saw that Eugenia did not dismiss the young men, he took his seat on a chair facing her, and made his request for her hand in words which it cost him an effort to make few and simple, for he kept his eyes fixed immovably upon her, and beheld her great beauty.

Eugenia smiled imperceptibly, and never even blushed, so tightly had learning and culture fettered all the finer impulses of ordinary life in her. Instead, she assumed a serious, profound expression, and made answer to him, "Thy wish, O Aquilinus, to have me for thy wife, honours me in a high degree, but is powerless to induce me to an act of unwisdom; and such it would justly be termed, if we were to follow the first crude impulse without examining ourselves. The first condition which I have to demand from a husband, whoever he be, is that he understand and honour and participate in my intellectual life and aims. So thou wilt be welcome to me if thou choosest to be often in my society, and to exercise thyself in emulation with these my young companions in the investigation of the highest things along with me. By this means we shall not fail to ascertain whether we are suited for each other or not, and, after a period of intellectual activity in common, we shall know each other so as beseems god-created beings who are meant to walk not in the darkness, but in the light."

To this high-flown demand Aquilinus answered, not without secret indignation, but still with proud tranquillity, "If I did not know thee, Eugenia, I would not desire thee for my wife; and, as to myself, great Rome knows me, as well as this province. If thy learning does not suffice to recognize what I am by this time, I fear it will never suffice. Besides, I did not come here to go to school again, but to find a helpmeet; and, as for these two children, my first request, if thou gavest me thy hand, would be that thou wouldest let them go and restore them to their parents at last, that they might help them and be of use to them.

Now I entreat thee, give me thy decision, not as a person of learning, but as a woman of flesh and blood!"

This time the fair she-philosopher had indeed turned red, red as a carnation, and said with fast-beating heart, "My answer is soon given, for I gather from thy words that thou dost not love me, Aquilinus. That might be a matter of indifference to me, were it not an outrage for the daughter of a noble Roman to be lied to!"

"I never lie!" said Aquilinus coldly. "Farewell!"

Eugenia turned her back without returning his farewell, and Aquilinus walked slowly out of the house to his own abode. She tried to take up her books as if nothing had happened; but the letters grew blurred before her eyes, and the two Hyacinths had to read to her while she, full of hot indignation, wandered with her thoughts elsewhere.

For, although up to that day she had regarded the consul as the only one among all her suitors whom she might have taken for a husband, supposing she had been so inclined, he was now become a stone of stumbling which she could not get over.

Aquilinus for his part attended calmly to his affairs of state, and sighed in secret over his strange folly, which would not suffer him to forget the pedantic beauty.

Almost two years passed, during which Eugenia became, if possible, more and more notable and a positively brilliant personage, while the two Hyacinths were now two sturdy rustic figures with growing beards. Although people everywhere began to take notice of this strange attachment, and, instead of the admiring epigrams, others in a more satiric vein began to appear, still she could not bring herself to part with her body-guard; for Aquilinus, who had presumed to order her to do so, was still there. He went quietly on his own way, and appeared to concern himself no more about her; but he looked at no other woman, and no other wooing was heard of, so that he also came in for censure, because, being so high an official, he remained unmarried.

Eugenia refrained all the more obstinately from offering any outward sign of reconciliation by dismissing her obnoxious companions. Besides, she was charmed to set ordinary custom and public opinion at defiance and be responsible to herself alone, and to preserve the consciousness of a pure life in circumstances which would have been perilous and impossible for any other woman.

Such eccentricities were in the air just at that time.

All the time Eugenia felt herself anything but well and happy. Her well-trained servitors must needs philosophize through heaven and earth and hell, only to be suddenly interrupted and forced to wander about in the country with her for hours together without being favoured with a single word. One day she was seized with the desire to make an excursion to a country-seat. She herself drove the carriage, and was in an amiable mood, for it was a bright spring day, and the air was full of balmy fragrance. The Hyacinths were delighted at her good humour. So they made their way through a country suburb where the Christians were permitted to hold their worship. They were in the act of celebrating Sunday; from the chapel of a monastery came the tones of a devout hymn. Eugenia checked her horses to listen, and caught the words of the psalm, "Like as the hart desireth the water-brooks: so longeth my soul after thee, O God. My soul is athirst for the living God."

At the sound of these words, sung by humble pious lips, her artificial life was made simple at last; her heart was touched, and seemed to realize what it desired; and slowly, without a word, she went on her way to the country-house. There she secretly put on men's clothes, signed to the two Hyacinths to come with her, and left the house unobserved by the menials. She went back to the convent, knocked at the door, and presented herself and her companions to the abbot as three young men who desired to be received into the convent that they might bid farewell to the world and live for eternity. Thanks to her good training, she was able to answer the abbot's searching questions so cleverly that he received all three, whom he could not help taking for refined and distinguished persons, into the convent, and permitted them to assume the monastic habit.

Eugenia made a beautiful, almost angelic, monk, and was called Brother Eugenius, while the two Hyacinths found themselves transformed for better or worse into monks; for they were never even consulted, and they had long been accustomed only to live according to the will of their female paragon. Still, they did not find the monkish life amiss; they enjoyed incomparably more peaceful days, did not require to study any more, and found no difficulty in surrendering themselves entirely to a passive obedience.

Brother Eugenius, on the other hand, did not remain idle, but became a notable monk, his visage white as marble, but with glowing eyes and the presence of an archangel. He converted many heathen, tended the sick and destitute, became profound in the Scriptures, preached in a golden bell-like voice, and on the abbot's death was actually chosen to be his successor. So now the tender Eugenia became abbot over seventy good monks, great and small.

During the time that she and her companions were thus mysteriously vanished and were nowhere to be found, her father had made enquiries at an oracle as to what had become of his daughter, and it answered that Eugenia had been taken away by the gods and placed among the stars. For the priests utilized the event

12

to contrive a miracle as a counterblast to the Christians, who all the time had the bird safely caged. They went so far as to point out a star in the firmament with two smaller stars adjacent as the new constellation, and the Alexandrians stood in the streets and on their house-tops to gaze at it, while many, who had formerly seen her going in and out, recalled her beauty, became enamoured of her memory, and looked up with moist eyes to the star, which swam placidly in the purple sky.

Aquilinus too looked up; but he shook his head and was not altogether satisfied about the business. The father of the vanished maiden was all the more obstinate in his credence, felt himself not a little exalted, and contrived, with the support of the priests, to have a statue erected and divine honours decreed to Eugenia. Aquilinus, from whom official sanction had to be obtained, granted it subject to the condition that the image should be made an exact likeness of the ravished one. That was easily accomplished, as there was quite a collection of busts and portraits of her in existence, and so her statue in marble was set up in the fore-court of the temple of Minerva, and challenged the inspection of gods and mortals, for, in spite of being a speaking likeness, it was an ideal work in features, pose, and drapery.

When this news was discussed among the seventy monks of the convent, they were bitterly chagrined at the trump card played by the heathen, as well as at the erection of a new idol and the shameless worship of a mortal woman. Their most violent objurgations were showered upon the woman herself as a runagate and juggling impostor, and they made a most unaccustomed noise during their midday meal. The Hyacinths, who had become two good little priestlings and had their abbot's secret concealed in their hearts, glanced significantly towards him, but he signed to them to keep silence, and suffered the outcry and abuse to pass as a penance for his former heathenish sinful mind.

But when that night was half run, Eugenia rose from her couch, took a heavy hammer, and went softly out of the convent to find the statue and break it in pieces. She easily found her way to the quarter of the city, all glistening with marble, where the temples and public buildings were situated, and where she had passed her youth. Not a soul stirred in the silent world of marble. Just as the female monk ascended the steps to the temple, the moon rose above the shadows of the city, and cast her beams as bright as day among the pillars of the fore-court. There Eugenia saw her statue, white as new-fallen snow, standing in wonderful grace and beauty, the finely-folded draperies chastely drawn over the shoulders, and looking straight forward with rapt eye and gently-smiling mouth.

Full of curiosity the Christian advanced towards it, the hammer uplifted in her hand; but a sweet shudder went through her heart when she obtained a clear view of the statue. She let the hammer sink, and breathlessly fed her gaze on the vision of her own former existence. A bitter regret took possession of her, a feeling as if she had been thrust out of a fairer world and was now wandering an unhappy shade in the wilderness. For although the image was elevated to the ideal, still the very ideal represented Eugenia's genuine inner nature, which had only been obscured by her pedantry, and it was a nobler emotion than vanity which now led her to recognize her better self by the magical moonlight. She suddenly felt as if she had played the wrong card--to use a modern expression; for, of course, there were no cards in those days.

Suddenly the quick step of a man was heard. Eugenia hid herself involuntarily in the shadow of a pillar, and saw the tall form of Aquilinus approaching. She saw how he stationed himself before the statue, gazed long upon it, and finally flung his arm about its neck to imprint a light kiss upon the marble lips. Then he wrapped himself in his mantle and slowly departed, more than once turning round to gaze at the gleaming image. Eugenia trembled so violently that she could feel her agitation. Full of wrath and violence, she gathered herself together and once again advanced toward the statue with uplifted hammer to make an end of the sinful maumet; but, instead of shattering the beauteous head, she burst into tears as she too imprinted a kiss upon its lips, then hastened away, for she could hear the steps of the night-watch. With heaving bosom, she slipped into her cell, and slept none that night until the sun arose, when, absenting herself from early prayers, she dreamt in rapid succession of things which had nothing in common with her devotions.

The monks respected their abbot's sleep as the result of spiritual vigils. But at last they were obliged to interrupt Eugenia's slumbers, as there was important business for her to attend to. A widow of rank, who professed to be lying sick and in need of Christian aid, had sent requesting the ghostly comfort and counsel of abbot Eugenius, whose deeds and person she had long revered. The monks did not wish to let slip this conquest, which would help the fame of their church, and they wakened Eugenia. Half dazed, with handsomely reddened cheeks, such as she had not been seen with for many a day, she set out, her thoughts in her morning dreams and the pillars of the midnight temple rather than in the business before her. She entered the heathen lady's house, and was conducted to her room and left alone with her. A beautiful woman, not yet thirty years old, was lying stretched upon a couch; but, so far from being sick and contrite, she was full of assurance and vitality. She could scarcely behave herself with bare quietness and modesty until the supposed monk, at her direction, had taken his seat close beside her; then she caught both his white hands, pressed her brow upon them, and covered them with kisses. Eugenia, who, absorbed in far other thoughts, had not observed the woman's unsaintly appearance, and had taken her behaviour for humility and pious devotion, let her have her way; and the

14

heathen, thus encouraged, flung her arms about Eugenia's neck, imagining that she was embracing the handsomest of young monks. In short, before he was aware, he found himself clasped tight by the amorous creature, and felt his mouth the target for a storm of passionate kisses. Completely dumbfounded, Eugenia awoke at last from her reverie; and even then it was some minutes before she could disengage herself from that wild embrace and rise to her feet.

But at the same instant the heathen Satan's tongue began to wag. In a storm of words the she-devil declared her love and desire to the indignant abbot, and sought by all manner of means to impress upon him that it was the duty of his youth and loveliness to assuage her desires, and that he was there for no other purpose. She did not fail to accompany her words with fresh assaults and tender allurements, so that Eugenia was scarcely able to defend herself. At last she rallied herself in indignation, and with flaming eyes read the shameless woman such a lesson and so answered her with such vigorous denunciations as only a monk has at command, that the latter recognized that her wicked intentions had failed, changed her tone in a twinkling, and took the way of escape which was once taken by Potiphar's wife, and has been taken a hundred and a thousand times since. She sprang like a tigress on Eugenia, clasped her again with arms like steel, pulled her down to her upon the couch, and at the same time set up such an outcry that her maids came running into the room from all quarters.

"Help! Help!" she screamed. "This man will force me!" And at the same time she released Eugenia, who got to her feet breathless, confused and horrified.

The women who had rushed to the rescue straightway screamed more desperately than their mistress, hastened hither and thither, and called for male assistance. Eugenia could not utter a word for horror; but made her escape from the house full of shame and disgust, followed by the outcries and curses of the infuriated rabble.

The fiendish widow lost no time in proceeding at once with a goodly following to the consul Aquilinus, and accusing the monk of the most disgraceful crime, to wit that he had come hypocritically to her house, first of all to molest her with efforts for her conversion, and, when these failed, to rob her of her honour by violence. Since all her following testified to the truth of her assertion, the indignant Aquilinus immediately caused the convent to be surrounded by troops, and the abbot along with his monks to be brought before him for trial.

"Is this what you do, you low hypocrites?" he said in severe tones. "Are you so high-fed, you who are barely tolerated, that you must needs assault our women-folk, and prowl about like ravening wolves? Did your Master, whom I honour more than I do you liars, teach or command you such things? Not at all! You are a gang, a horde of wretches, who assume a name in public that you may abandon yourselves to corruption in secret. Defend yourselves against the charge, if you can!"

The infamous widow then repeated her lying tale, interrupted by hypocritical sighs and tears. When she had finished and had wrapped herself again demurely in her veil, the monks glanced fearfully at one another and at their abbot, of whose virtue they had no doubt, and they raised their voices with one accord to repel the false accusation. But not only the numerous menials of the lying woman, but also several neighbours and passers-by, who had seen the abbot leaving the house full of shame and confusion and who had thereupon taken him for guilty, now came forward and testified one after the other with loud voices to the fact of the crime, so that the poor monks were shouted down ten times over.

Now they glanced once more, this time full of doubt, at their abbot, and his very youth suddenly appeared suspicious to the greybeards among them. They exclaimed that, if he were guilty, God's judgement would not be backward, no more than they were backward in abandoning him there and then to the secular arm!

The eyes of all were now directed upon Eugenia, who stood forsaken amid the throng. She had been lying weeping in her cell when she was arrested with the monks, and had stood all that time, her eyes downcast and her cowl drawn deep down over her head, and felt herself in a most awkward predicament. For, if she preserved the secret of her family and sex, she would succumb to this false testimony, while, if she revealed it, the storm would break out against the convent more furiously than ever, and she would devote it to destruction, since a convent which had a beautiful young woman for abbot was bound to become the butt of the most unholy suspicion and mockery on the part of the malicious heathen world. She would not have experienced this timidity and indecision had she still had a pure heart, according to monkish notions; but the events of the previous night had already made a division in her mind, and her unfortunate encounter with the wicked woman had only increased her wavering, so that she no longer possessed the courage to step forward with determination and bring about a miracle.

Yet, when Aquilinus called upon her to speak, she remembered his former tenderness for her, and, as she had confidence in him, she hit upon a way of escape. In gentle and modest tones she said that she was not guilty and would prove it to the consul, if she might speak with him alone. The sound of her voice moved Aquilinus, though he knew not why, and he acceded to her request to speak with him in private. He accordingly had her conducted into his house, and repaired alone with her into a room. Then Eugenia fixed her eyes upon him, threw back her cowl and said, "I am Eugenia, whom you once desired for your wife."

He recognized her at once, and was convinced that it was she; but at the same time a great anger and a burning jealousy rose up within his breast to think that the lost one so suddenly recovered should make her appearance as a woman who had been living all that time in secrecy with seventy monks. He therefore restrained himself with a violent effort and scrutinized her narrowly, while he made as if he did not believe her assertion in the slightest, and said, "You certainly do seem rather like that infatuated young woman. But that does not concern me; I am much more anxious to know what you did to the widow!"

Eugenia shyly and anxiously told all that had passed, and from the whole tone of her story Aquilinus perceived the falsehood and malice of the accusation, yet he answered with apparent indifference, "But if you are Eugenia, then how did you contrive to become a monk? What was your intention, and how was it possible?"

At these words, Eugenia blushed and looked on the ground in embarrassment. Still, it seemed to her not so unpleasant after all to be there, and to be talking once again with a good old acquaintance about herself and her adventures. So she lost no time, but told in unstudied words all that had happened to her since her disappearance, except, strangely enough, that she never uttered a syllable about the two Hyacinths. Her hearer found the story not unsatisfactory, only every minute made it harder for him to conceal his appreciation of the recovered fair one. But nevertheless he controlled himself, and determined to see the matter out to the end and to ascertain from her subsequent behaviour whether he had the old Eugenia before him, with her chaste and pure manners.

So he said, "All that is a well told story: still, in spite of her eccentricities, I do not consider that the maiden you pretend to be was capable of such very astonishing adventures. At least, the real Eugenia would certainly have preferred to become a nun. For how in the world can a monk's cowl and living among seventy monks be a merit and salvation for any woman, even the most learned and pious? No, I still hold to my opinion that you are a smooth-faced beardless fellow of an impostor, whom I don't trust in the slightest! Besides, Eugenia has been proclaimed as deified and dwelling among the stars; her image stands where it was dedicated in the temple, and it will go hard enough with you if you persist in your slanderous assertion."

"A certain man kissed that image last night," retorted Eugenia in a low voice, casting a curious look at the disconcerted Aquilinus, who gazed upon her as upon one inspired with superhuman wisdom. "How can the same man torture the original?"

But he mastered his confusion, appeared not to hear her words, and continued, coldly and severely, "In one word, for the honour of the poor Christian monks, who appear to me to be innocent, I cannot and will not believe that you are a woman. Prepare yourself for judgement, for your statements have not satisfied me."

At that Eugenia exclaimed, "Then God help me!" and, rending her monk's frock in twain, pale as a white rose, she collapsed in shame and despair. But Aquilinus caught her in his arms, pressed her to his heart, and wrapped her in his mantle, while his tears fell upon her lovely head; for he was convinced that she was an honourable woman. He carried her into the next room, where there was a richly furnished guest-bed, laid her gently down in it and covered her to the chin with purple coverlets. Then he kissed her on the lips, perhaps three or four times, went out, and locked the door securely. Next he picked up the monk's frock, which lay still warm on the floor, and betook himself again to the waiting throng outside, and addressed them thus, "These are strange happenings! You monks are innocent and may go to your convent. Your abbot was a demon who would have ruined you or seduced you. Here! Take his frock with you and hang it somewhere for a memorial; for, after he had changed his form in the oddest fashion before my eyes, he dissolved into nothing before these same eyes, and vanished without a trace. As for this woman of whom the demon made use in order to ruin you, she is under suspicion of witchcraft and must be put in prison. Now begone all of you to your homes, and behave yourselves!"

All were astounded at this allocution, and gazed fearfully at the demon's garment. The widow turned pale and veiled her face, and by so doing made ample betrayal of her bad conscience. The good monks rejoiced over their victory and retired most thankfully with the empty husk, little suspecting what a sweet kernel had been hidden within it. The widow was cast into prison, and Aquilinus summoned his most faithful servant and went through the city, sought out merchants, and purchased a perfect load of the most expensive female attire, which the slave had to convey to the house as secretly and quickly as possible.

Softly the consul slipped into the chamber where Eugenia lay, seated himself on the edge of her bed, and saw that she was sleeping quite contentedly, like one recovering from difficulties undergone. He could not help laughing at the black pile of her shorn monk's head, and passed a gentle hand over the thick, short hair. Thereupon she awoke and opened her eyes.

"Will you be my wife now, at last?" he enquired gently; whereupon she said neither Yes nor No, but shivered a little beneath the purple coverlets in which she lay wrapped.

Then Aquilinus brought in all the clothes and ornaments that a fine lady required in those days to array herself from head to foot, and left her.

After sundown that same day, he took her with him, attended only by his faithful servant, to one of his country-houses, which lay in a secluded and charming situation amid the shade of thick trees.

In the country-house, the pair now celebrated their nuptials with the utmost privacy; and, for as long as it had been until they found each other again, still no time seemed to have been lost, rather they felt the most hearty thankfulness for the good fortune which had preserved them for each other. Aquilinus devoted the days to his official business, and at night drove as fast as horses could take him home to his wife. Only now and again on unkindly, stormy, wet days, he loved to hasten back earlier than he was expected to the country-house to cheer Eugenia.

Without making many words about it, she now devoted herself to the study of connubial love and fidelity, with the same thoroughness and perseverance which she had formerly spent upon philosophy and Christian discipline. But, when her hair had grown again to its proper length, Aquilinus, having devised a cunning fable, took his spouse at last back to Alexandria, brought her to her astonished parents, and celebrated a brilliant wedding.

Her father was certainly surprised to find his daughter again, not as an immortal goddess and a heavenly constellation, but as a beloved, earthly, wedded wife, and it was with regret that he saw the consecrated statue removed from the temple; but, to his praise, his disappointment was overcome by his fondness for his living daughter, who now proved fairer and more lovable than ever. The marble statue Aquilinus set in the finest room in his house; but he refrained from kissing it again, now that he had the warm, living original to his hand.

After Eugenia had investigated the nature of marriage to her satisfaction, she applied her experience to converting her spouse to Christianity, which she still continued to profess; and she did not rest until Aquilinus had made public acknowledgement of his adhesion to her faith. The legend goes on to relate how the whole family returned to Rome about the time when that enemy of the Christians, Valerian, came to the throne; and how, during the persecutions which then broke out, Eugenia added to her fame that of a famous heroine of the faith and martyr, and then only made full manifestation of her great strength of soul.

Her influence over Aquilinus had become so great that she was able to bring the two clerics, the Hyacinths, with her from Alexandria to Rome, where they also won the martyr's crown at the same time as she. Her intercession is said to be specially efficacious for dull school-girls who are backward in their studies.

THE VIRGIN AND THE DEVIL

Friend! watch and look about, the Devil is always prowling;
If thou triest a bout with him, thou'lt get a thorough towelling.
Angelus Silesius, *Cherub. Wandersmann*, Book vi. 206.

There was a certain Count Gebizo, who possessed a wondrously beautiful wife, a magnificent castle and town, and so many valuable possessions that he was esteemed one of the richest and most fortunate nobles in the country. He seemed to be aware of and thankful for his reputation, for he not only kept a splendid and hospitable board, at which his fair and virtuous wife warmed the hearts of his guests like a sun, but he also practised Christian beneficence in the most comprehensive fashion.

He founded and endowed convents and hospitals, beautified churches and chapels, and on every high-day gave clothing, meat and drink to a great number, often hundreds, of poor; and several dozen must needs be seen every day, almost every hour, about his courtyard, regaling themselves and praising him, otherwise his dwelling, fair as it was, would have seemed to him deserted.

But by such unbounded liberality even the greatest wealth is exhausted, and so it came to pass that the Count was obliged to mortgage all his properties one after the other in order to indulge his passion for grandiose beneficence; and the more he got into debt the more eagerly he redoubled his almsgiving and feasts to the poor, hoping thereby, as he imagined, to turn the blessing of Heaven once more in his favour. In the end he impoverished himself entirely; his castle became deserted and ruinous; ineffective and foolish foundations and deeds of gift, which from force of habit he could not desist from writing, brought him nothing but ridicule; and any tattered beggar, whom he might now and again lure to his castle, threw the meagre pittance at his benefactor's feet, and took himself off with scornful words of abuse.

One thing only was left to him unimpaired, the beauty of his wife Bertrade; nay, the barer things looked in the house, the more brilliant did her beauty seem to grow. She increased too in grace, love and goodness the poorer Gebizo became, so that all the blessings of Heaven seemed to be comprehended in his wife, and thousands of men envied the Count this one treasure which still remained to him. He alone was blind to all this, and the more the fair Bertrade exerted herself to cheer him and sweeten his poverty the less he prized that jewel, and he fell into a bitter and obstinate dejection and hid himself from the world.

One day, when a glorious Easter-morning dawned, a day on which he had once been wont to see joyous throngs making pilgrimage to his castle, he felt so

20

ashamed of his downfall that he had not even heart to go to church, and was perplexed how to pass the bright sunny feast-days. In vain his wife, with pearly tears and smiling lips, begged him not to vex himself, but come with her to church undismayed; he tore himself away crossly, and took himself off to hide in the woods until Easter were over.

Up hill and down dale he wandered, until he came to a primeval wilderness, where monstrous bearded firs surrounded a lake whose depths reflected the gloomy trees in all their length so that everything looked dismal and black. The ground about the lake was thickly carpeted with strange long-fringed moss, in which no footfall could be heard.

Here Gebizo sat himself down and complained to God of his wretched ill fortune, which no longer enabled him to still his own hunger sufficiently, his who had once gladly satisfied thousands, and, worst of all, which recompensed his efforts with the scorn and ingratitude of the world.

On a sudden he observed in the middle of the lake a skiff, and in it a man of lofty stature. As the lake was small and one could easily see across it, Gebizo could not comprehend where the boatman could have come from so suddenly, for he had not observed him anywhere before. Enough, he was now there, gave one stroke of his oar and immediately was on the shore beside the knight, and, before the latter could give a thought to the affair, had enquired of him why he turned such a rueful face to the world. In spite of his extremely handsome exterior, the stranger had an expression of deep-seated discontent about his mouth and eyes; yet this was the very thing which gained Gebizo's confidence, and without any reserve he poured out the tale of his misfortunes and grievances.

"You are a fool," the other responded, "for you possess a treasure greater than all that you have lost. If I had your wife, I should never give a thought to all the riches and churches and convents, nor to all the beggar-folk in the world."

"Give me back those things, and you are welcome to my wife in exchange!" retorted Gebizo with a bitter laugh, and the other exclaimed quick as lightning. "A bargain! Look under your wife's pillow; there you will find what will suffice for all your lifetime to build a convent every day, and feed a thousand people, though you should live to a hundred. In exchange, bring me your wife here to this spot without fail the evening before Walpurgis!"

With these words, such a fire spurted from his dark eyes that two reddish beams glanced over the Count's sleeve, and thence over moss and fir-trees. Then Gebizo saw whom he had before him, and accepted the man's offer. The latter plied his oar, and sailed back to the middle of the lake, where he and his boat sank into the water with a din which resembled the laughter of many brazen bells.

21

Gebizo, all in a goose-skin, hastened back by the nearest way to his castle, searched Bertrade's bed at once, and found under her pillow an old, shabby book which he could not decipher. But, as he turned over the leaves, one gold piece after another fell out. As soon as he observed this, he betook himself with the book to the deepest vault of a tower, and there, in the utmost secrecy, set to work and spent all the rest of Easter in turning out an ample heap of gold from the pages of this most interesting work.

Then he appeared in the world once again, redeemed all his possessions, summoned workmen who restored his castle more magnificently than ever, and dispensed benefactions on every hand like a prince who has been newly crowned. The principal of his works, however, was the foundation of a great abbey for five hundred capitulars of the utmost piety and distinction, a regular town of saints and scholars, in the centre of which his burial-place was one day to be. He considered this provision requisite for his eternal salvation. But, as his wife was otherwise provided for, no burial-place was prepared for her.

The midday before Walpurgis he gave the order to saddle, and bade his fair wife mount her white hunter, as she had a long journey to ride in his company. At the same time he forbade a single squire or servant to attend them. A great dread seized the poor woman; she trembled in every limb, and for the first time in her life she lied to her husband, pretending that she was unwell, and begging him to leave her at home. As she had been singing to herself only a little time before, Gebizo was incensed at the falsehood, and considered that he had now acquired a double right over her. She was forced therefore to mount her horse, dressed too in her best finery, and she rode away sadly with her husband, not knowing whither she was going.

When they had accomplished about half their journey, they came to a little church which Bertrade had happened to build in former days and had dedicated to the Mother of God. She had done it for the sake of a poor master-mason whom no one would employ, because he was so surly and disagreeable, that even Gebizo, whom others could not help approaching in a pleasant and respectful fashion, could not tolerate him, and sent him away empty-handed, for all the work which he had to give out. She had caused the little church to be built secretly, and in his gratitude the despised master-mason had with his own hands wrought a remarkably beautiful image of Mary in his spare time, and set it over the altar.

Bertrade now craved to enter this church for a moment and say her prayers, and Gebizo allowed her; for he thought she might have much need of them. So she dismounted from her horse, and, while her husband waited outside, went in, knelt before the altar, and commended herself to the protection of the Virgin Mary. Thereupon she fell into a deep sleep; the Virgin sprang down from the altar, assumed the form and garments of the sleeper, went gaily out by the door and mounted the horse, on which she continued the journey at Gebizo's side and in Bertrade's stead.

The wretch thought to continue to deceive his wife, and, the nearer they came to the journey's end, to lull her and hoodwink her by an increase of friendliness. Accordingly he talked with her of this and that, and the Virgin chatted pleasantly and gave him confiding answers, and behaved as if she had lost all her timidity. So they reached the gloomy wilderness about the lake, over which dun evening clouds hung; the ancient firs bloomed purple with buds, as only happens in the most luxuriant spring-tides; in the thicket a ghostly nightingale sang as loud as organ-pipes and cymbals; and out from among the fir-trees rode the man ye wot of, mounted on a black stallion, in rich knightly array, with a long sword at his side.

He approached very courteously, although he suddenly shot such a ferocious look at Gebizo that his flesh crept; still, the horses did not appear to scent anything dangerous, for they stood quiet. Trembling, Gebizo flung his wife's reins to the stranger and galloped off alone without so much as a glance back to her. But the stranger grasped the reins with a hasty hand, and away they went like a whirlwind through the firs, so that the fair rider's veil and garments fluttered and waved, away over mountain and valley, and over the flowing waters so that the horses' hoofs scarcely touched the foam of their waves. Hurried along by the boisterous storm, a rosy, fragrant cloud, which shone in the twilight, was wafted in front of the steeds; and the nightingale flew invisible before the pair, settling here and there upon a tree and singing until the air rang again.

At last all hills and all trees came to an end, and the two rode into an endless heath, in the midst of which, as if from afar off, the nightingale throbbed, although there was no sign of bush or bough on which it could have sat.

Suddenly the rider halted, sprang from his horse, and helped the lady out of the saddle with the manner of a perfect cavalier. Scarcely had her foot touched the heath, when round about the pair there sprang up a garden of rose-bushes as tall as a man, with a splendid fountain and seat, above which a starry firmament shone so brilliantly that one could have seen to read by its light. But the fountain consisted of a great round basin in which, like modern *tableaux vivants*, a number of devils formed, or represented, a seductive group of nymphs in white marble. They poured shimmering water from their hollowed hands--whence they got it, their lord and master only knew. The water made the most lovely harmony; for every jet gave out a different note, and the whole seemed in concert like string-music. It was, so to say, a water-harmonica, whose chords were thrilled through and through with all the deliciousness of that first night of

May, and melted into unison with the charming forms of the group of nymphs; for the living picture did not stand still, but changed and turned imperceptibly.

Not without tender emotion, the strange cavalier conducted the lady to the seat and invited her to be seated; but then he gripped her hand with a violent tenderness, and said in a voice that pierced to the marrow, "I am the Eternally Forlorn who fell from Heaven! Nothing but the love of a good mortal woman on May-night can make me forget Paradise and give me strength to endure my eternal discomfiture. Be but my helpmeet, and I will make thee eternal, and grant thee the power of doing good and preventing evil to thy heart's content!"

He flung himself passionately on the bosom of the beauteous woman, who smilingly opened her arms. But at the same instant the Blessed Virgin assumed her Heavenly form, and enclosed the entrapped Deceiver in her radiant arms with all her might. In a twinkling, the garden had vanished with its fountain and nightingale; the cunning demons, who had formed the tableau, took flight in the form of evil spirits, uttering cries of anguish, and left their lord in the lurch; while he, never uttering a sound, wrestled with titanic strength to free himself from the torturing embrace.

But the Virgin held on bravely and did not let him go, though indeed she had to summon all her strength. She purposed nothing less than to bring the outmanoeuvred Devil before Heaven, and there expose him bound to a gate-post in all his wretchedness to the laughter of the blessed.

But the Evil One changed his tactics, kept still for a brief space, and assumed the beauty which he had once possessed as the fairest among the angels, so that he almost rivalled the celestial beauty of Mary. She exalted herself as much as possible; yet, if she was radiant as Venus the fair Evening-star, he shone like Lucifer the Son of the Morning, so that it began to be as bright on that dusky heath as if the heavens themselves had descended upon it.

When the Virgin perceived that she had undertaken too much, and that her strength was failing, she contented herself with releasing the Fiend on condition that he renounced the Count's wife, and the celestial and infernal beauties forthwith separated with great violence. The Virgin, somewhat wearied, betook herself back to her little church; the Evil One, incapable of any further disguise and mauled in every limb, crawled away over the sand in horrid, degraded form, the very embodiment of long-tailed sorrow. So badly had his purposed hour of dalliance turned out for him.

Meantime Gebizo, after abandoning his lovely wife, had gone astray in the darkening night, and horse and rider had fallen into a chasm, where his head was dashed against a stone so that he promptly departed this life.

As for Bertrade, she remained in her sleep until the sun rose on the first of May; then she awoke, and was surprised to see how the time had flown. Still, she quickly said her Ave Maria, and, when she came out of the church hale and hearty, her horse was standing before the door as she had left it. She did not wait long for her husband, but rode home blithely and quickly, for she guessed that she had escaped from some great peril.

Soon the Count's body was found and brought home. Bertrade had it entombed with all honour, and founded innumerable masses for him. But all love for him was in some inexplicable way eradicated from her heart, although it remained as kind and tender as ever. Accordingly, her exalted patroness in Heaven looked about for another husband for her, who should be more worthy of such gracious love than the deceased Gebizo had been. How this business came about is written in the next legend.

THE VIRGIN AS KNIGHT

Mary is named a Throne, the Lord's own Tabernacle,
An Ark, Keep, Tower, House, a Spring, Tree, Garden, Mirror,
A Sea, a Star, the Moon, a Hill, the Blush of Morning.
All these how can she be? She is another world!
Angelus Silesius, *Cherub. Wandersmann*, Book iv. 42.

Gebizo had acquired so much wealth over and above his former possessions that Bertrade found herself mistress of a noble earldom, and became famous throughout the Empire for her wealth as well as her beauty. As, withal, she was very unassuming and friendly with every one, the jewel of her person appeared an easy conquest to all the nobility, shy and enterprising, bold and timid, great and small alike, and every one who had seen her a few times was surprised that he did not already have her in his possession. Yet more than a year passed, and no one knew of any who had acquired real grounds for hope.

Even the Emperor heard of her, and, as he was desirous that such a splendid fief should pass into the hands of a suitable husband, he determined to pay the celebrated widow a visit in the course of a journey, and signified his intention to her in a most gracious and friendly letter. This he entrusted to a young knight Zendelwald, whose road lay that way. He was favourably received by Bertrade, and entertained handsomely, as was every one who resorted to her castle. He beheld with admiration the lordly halls, battlements and gardens, and incidentally fell violently in love with their mistress. Still, he did not linger an hour longer in the castle on that account; but, when he had delivered his message and seen all that there was to see, he took a brief farewell of the lady and rode away, the only one of all those who had ever been there who did not think himself competent to win that prize.

The fact was that he was sluggish in word and deed. Even when his mind and heart had mastered any matter, which they always did with thoroughness and fire, Zendelwald could never bring himself to take the first step to a realization, for the thing seemed to him as good as finished when once he saw his way clearly to it in his mind. Although he was ready enough to talk when there was nothing to be gained by doing so, he never uttered the opportune word which would have brought him fortune. Not only his tongue, but his hand too, was so far behind his thought that in battle he was often all but overcome by his opponent, because, seeing in his mind's eye his enemy already at his feet, he delayed giving the decisive stroke. Thus his manner of fighting excited surprise at every tournament; for he always began by scarcely exerting himself, and it was not until he was in the utmost extremity that he gained the victory by some masterly stroke.

His mind in full play on the subject of the fair Bertrade, our Zendelwald now rode home to his little castle, which lay in a lonely mountain forest. A few charcoal-burners and woodmen were all his subjects, and so his mother always awaited his return in bitter impatience to know whether he had at last brought home fortune.

Zendelwald's mother was as handy and determined as he was indolent, though not any more successful; for on her side she had carried her qualities to excess, and they had twined into fussiness. In her youth she had been eager to find a husband as soon as possible, and had overpressed several opportunities so hastily and eagerly that in her haste she had made the very worst possible choice in the shape of a disreputable, foolhardy fellow, who ran through all his inheritance, came to a premature end, and left her nothing but a long widowhood, poverty and one son who would not take the trouble to bestir himself to grasp at fortune.

The little household's only fare consisted of the milk of some goats, forest-fruits, and game. Zendelwald's mother was an accomplished sportswoman, and shot wild pigeons and grouse with the cross-bow as she pleased. She also caught trout in the brooks, and with her own hands repaired the little castle with stone and lime where it became decayed. At that moment she had just returned home with a hare which she had knocked over, and, as she hung the animal from the window of her high-perched kitchen, she gave another look out into the valley and saw her son riding along the road. She let down the drawbridge with joy, for he had been absent for months.

She at once began to enquire whether he had got hold of any tuft or feather of luck to bring home and make the most of, and, as he recounted the usual unprofitable experiences of his most recent campaign, she shook her head in wrath. But, when he came to tell her all about his mission to the rich and captivating Bertrade, and lauded her kindness and beauty, she scolded him for a lazy-bones and a faint-heart to run away so basely. She was not long in perceiving that Zendelwald could think of nothing else than the far-off lady, and she began to be downright impatient with him to think that with such a praiseworthy passion in his heart he failed utterly to make anything of it, since in his case to be so head and ears over in love was a hindrance rather than an incentive to action.

His days were not of the happiest. His mother was sulky with him, and in her irritation sought to divert herself by mending the damaged roof of the tower, so that the good Zendelwald was in fear and trembling as he saw her clambering about aloft. In her ill temper she would pitch down broken tiles, and wellnigh knocked out the brains of a stranger knight as he was about to enter the door to request a night's lodging.

The latter, however, managed to win the ungracious lady's friendship during supper, as he related many pleasant things, and in particular that the Emperor was then staying at the pretty widow's great castle where one feast was followed by another, and the fortunate lady was unceasingly besieged by the Emperor and his lords to choose a husband from among them. She, however, had found a way of evasion by convoking a great tournament and promising her hand to the victor, in the firm belief that her patron the Blessed Virgin would intervene and direct the arm of the right man, who was destined for her, to victory.

"Now, that would be something for you to try," the guest concluded, turning to Zendelwald; "such a handsome young knight ought to go straight for it and try to win the best fortune of these days, according to worldly estimation. Besides, it is commonly said that the lady hopes that in this way some unknown luck may turn up, perchance some poor but honest hero, whom she can kiss and coll, and that she has an aversion to all the great and famous counts and idle wooers."

When the stranger had ridden away, Zendelwald's mother said, "Now, I'll wager that no less a person than Bertrade herself sent that messenger to put you on the right track, my dear Zendelwald! It's as clear as daylight; what other business had the fellow, who has drunk our last flagon of wine, to bring him travelling in this forest?"

Her son began to laugh mightily at her words, and went on laughing more and more heartily, partly at the manifest impossibility of his mother's fancies, partly

27

because he found those said fancies rather agreeable. The mere thought that Bertrade could possibly wish to take possession of him kept him laughing uncontrollably. But his mother, who thought that he was laughing in derision of her, flew into a rage, and cried, "Listen! My curse be upon you if you do not obey me and set out on your way at once to win that fortune. Do not come back without it, else I never wish to see you again! Or, if you do come back, I'll take my bow and arrows and go out to seek a grave where I can have peace from your stupidity!"

So now Zendelwald had no choice; for the sake of peace and quietness, he furbished his weapons, sighing the while, and rode as Heaven might guide him in the direction of Bertrade's dwelling, without being convinced that he should really go there. Nevertheless he stuck pretty close to the road, and the nearer he came to his destination, the more clearly the thought took shape that, after all, he might undertake the adventure as well as another, and that, when he had settled matters with his rivals, it would not cost him his head to try conclusions with the fair lady. The adventure now developed stage by stage in his mind, and came to the happiest issue; indeed, all day long, as he rode through the green summer landscape, he held sweet dialogues with his beloved, in which he told her most beautiful conceits, so that her face became rosy for gratification and joy--all this in his imagination.

As he was in the act of inwardly depicting one more happy event, he saw in good earnest, on a distant blue ridge, the towers and battlements of the castle shining in the morning sun, with its gilded balustrades gleaming from afar, and was so startled at the sight that all the fabric of his dreams was dissolved, and left nothing but a faint, irresolute heart behind.

Involuntarily he reined in his horse and looked around, as laggards will, for a place of refuge. Whereupon he became aware of a pretty little church, the same which Bertrade had once built to the Mother of God, and in which she had slept that sleep. He at once resolved to go in and collect his thoughts somewhat before the altar, the more so as it was the day on which the tournament was to be held.

The priest was in the act of singing Mass, which was attended only by two or three poor people, so that the knight contributed no small ornament to the little congregation. When all was over, and priest and sacristan had left the church, Zendelwald felt so comfortable in those quarters that he fell sound asleep, and forgot tournament and beloved one, unless indeed he dreamt about them.

Thereupon the Virgin Mary stepped down once again from her altar, assumed his form and accoutrements, mounted his horse, and rode with closed visor, a bold Brunhilda, all the way to the castle in Zendelwald's stead.

When she had ridden a while, she came across a heap of dried rubbish and withered brushwood lying by the wayside. It seemed suspicious to the watchful

Virgin, and she noticed something like the tail-end of a serpent peeping out of the confusion. She saw then that it was the Devil, who, still as enamoured as ever, was also prowling about the neighbourhood of the castle, and had hurriedly hid himself from the Virgin in the rubbish. She rode past without appearing to notice him, but cleverly made her horse spring to the side, so that he came down with his hind hoofs on the suspicious tail-end. With a hiss the Evil One made out and away, and never more showed himself again in this connection.

Amused by the little adventure, she rode, full of good humour, to Bertrade's castle, where she arrived just when only the two stoutest jousters remained to fight the deciding contest.

Slowly and carelessly, for all the world like Zendelwald, she rode into the lists, and appeared undecided whether she should take part in the contest or not.

"Here comes lazy Zendelwald," the word went round, and the two stout champions said, "What does he want with us? Just a minute, and let us get him out of the way before we settle matters between ourselves."

One of the champions called himself "Guhl the Speedy." He was in the habit of turning himself and his horse about like a whirlwind, and trying to bewilder and outwit his opponents by a hundred tricks and stratagems. The supposed Zendelwald had to engage him first. He wore a coal-black moustache, the ends of which were twisted and turned up in the air so stiffly that two little silver bells, which were attached to them, could not bend them down, and tinkled incessantly whenever he moved his head. He described this as a peal of terror for his foes and of delight for his lady! His shield glittered, now with this colour, now with that, according to the direction in which he turned it, and he could effect this change so rapidly that the eye was blinded by it. His plume was formed of an enormous cock's tail.

The other stout champion dubbed himself "Mouse the Innumerable," by which he meant to convey that he was as good as an innumerable army. In token of his prowess, he had allowed the hair of his nostrils to grow out about six inches, and had plaited it into two tresses, which hung over his mouth and were adorned at the ends with neat little red favours. Over his armour he wore a great spreading mantle, which almost enveloped himself and his horse, and was cunningly sewed together from a thousand mouseskins. For a crest, he was overshadowed by the mighty outspread wings of a bat, from under which he darted threatening glances out of his slits of eyes.

When the signal was given for the fight with Guhl the Speedy, he rode against the Virgin and encircled her with ever-increasing rapidity, seeking to dazzle her with his shield, and directing a hundred thrusts at her with his lance. All the time, the Virgin stuck to the same spot in the middle of the lists, and appeared to do no more than defend herself with shield and spear, skilfully turning her horse

29

about on its hind-legs so that she always presented her front to her opponent. When Guhl observed this, he suddenly rode some distance back, then turned and ran upon her with his lance in rest, intending to thrust her over the crupper. The Virgin awaited him without stirring; but man and horse seemed of bronze, so firm they stood, and the poor fellow, unaware that he was contending against superhuman power, flew unexpectedly out of his saddle, and lay upon the ground, when he ran upon her spear, while his own was shattered like a straw upon her shield. Without delay the Virgin dismounted, knelt on his breast so that he could not move under the mighty pressure, and with her dagger cut away his moustaches and their silver bells, and fastened them in her sword-belt, while fanfares proclaimed her, or rather Zendelwald, the victor.

Next, Sir Mouse the Innumerable came into the dance. He galloped forward with such violence that his mantle floated in the air like a threatening grey cloud. But the Virgin-Zendelwald, who only now appeared to be beginning to warm up to the fray, galloped as stoutly to meet him, threw him with ease from the saddle at the first thrust, and when Mouse rose at once and drew his sword, she dismounted at the same instant to engage him on foot. He was soon dazed by the rapid strokes with which her sword fell upon his head and shoulders, and he held out his mantle with his left hand to shelter beneath it, and wait a favourable opportunity to throw it over his opponent's head. At that, the Virgin caught a tip of the mantle with the point of her sword, and enveloped Mouse the Innumerable in it from head to foot so dexterously and swiftly that he was soon like an enormous wasp entangled in a spider's web, and lay struggling on the ground.

Then the Virgin belaboured him with the flat of her sword so vigorously that the mantle was resolved into its component parts, and a shower of mouse-skins darkened the air amid the universal laughter of the spectators, while the knight gradually emerged again to view, and limped away a beaten man, after his conqueror had cut away his beribboned pigtails.

Thus the Virgin under the guise of Zendelwald remained victor of the field.

She now opened her visor, strode up to the Queen of the Festival, and on bended knee laid the trophies of victory at her feet. Then she rose, and offered the spectacle of a Zendelwald such as he was usually too shy to be. Without, however, compromising his modesty too much, she greeted Bertrade with a look, whose effect on the female heart she well knew. In a word, she proved that she could play, not only the champion, but the lover, so well, that Bertrade did not take back her word, but lent a willing ear to the advice of the Emperor, who after all was glad to see so gallant and noble a man prevail.

Then there was a great festive procession to the gardens, with their tall lime-trees, where the banquet was spread. There Bertrade sat between the Emperor and her Zendelwald. But it was as well that the former was occupied with another pleasant lady; for the latter did not give his bride much time to converse with others, so politely and tenderly did he entertain her. He said the nicest things to her on the spur of the moment, so that time after time she reddened with pleasure. Joy and contentment prevailed everywhere; up in the green vault of the trees the birds sang, vying with the instruments of music; a butterfly settled on the Emperor's crown; and, as if by a special blessing, the wine-cups gave forth a fragrance like violets and mignonette.

But Bertrade, above all, felt so happy, that, while Zendelwald held her by the hand, she thought in her heart of her celestial protectress, and made her a fervent, silent thanksgiving.

The Virgin Mary, who all the time was sitting at her side as Zendelwald, read the prayer in her heart, and was so well pleased at her ward's pious gratitude that she embraced Bertrade tenderly, and imprinted a kiss on her lips, which, as may be imagined, filled the fair woman with heavenly bliss; for when the celestials take to baking sweet-stuff, it is sweet indeed.

As for the Emperor and the rest of the company, they shouted approval to the supposed Zendelwald, raised their goblets, and drank to the health of the handsome couple.

Meanwhile, the real Zendelwald waked out of his unseasonable sleep, and found the sun so far on its course that the tournament must certainly be over. Although he was now well out of the business, still he felt very unhappy and sad; for he would have been only too glad to wed the lady Bertrade. Besides, he did not dare to go back to his mother now. So he determined to set out on an endless, joyless wandering, until death should release him from his useless existence. Only, before doing so, he wished to see his beloved one once again, and imprint her image on his mind for the remainder of his days, that he might always remember what he had thrown away.

He accordingly went back all the way to the castle. When he reached the throng, he heard everywhere proclaimed the praises and good fortune of a poor knight Zendelwald who had attained the prize, and, bitterly curious to know who this fortunate namesake might be, he dismounted from his horse, and forced his way through the crowd until he found a station at the edge of the garden, on an elevated place from which he could overlook the whole feast.

There he beheld in all her finery, not far from the sparkling crown of the Emperor, the radiant, happy face of his beloved; but side by side with her--his astonishment turned him pale--the living image of his own person. As he stood petrified, he saw his double embrace and kiss the pious bride. Thereupon, without delay, he stepped, unnoticed amid the universal joy, through the ranks until he stood, racked by a strange jealousy, close behind the couple. At the

31

same moment, his counterfeit vanished from Bertrade's side, and she looked about for him in dismay. But when she saw Zendelwald behind her, she laughed joyfully, and said, "Where are you off to? Come, stay beside me!" And she took his hand and drew him to her side.

So he sat down, and, to test the seeming dream thoroughly, he seized the beaker which stood before him and emptied it at one draught. The wine stood the test, and an unmistakable life streamed through his veins. Quite in the mood, he turned to the smiling woman and looked into her eyes; whereupon she joyously resumed the intimate conversation which had been interrupted the moment before. But Zendelwald could not imagine what had happened to him, when he found Bertrade address him in familiar words, to which he several times unthinkingly answered in others which he had already used somewhere else. Sure enough he discovered after a little that his predecessor must have been carrying on the very same conversation with Bertrade which he had devised in his imagination during the days of his journey, and which he now continued deliberately, in order to see what end the play would have.

But it did not have an end. Instead, it became more and more edifying; for when the sun went down, torches were lighted, and the whole assembly made for the largest hall in the castle to engage in dancing. After the Emperor had danced the first round with the bride, Zendelwald took her on his arm and danced three or four times with her round the hall until, all aglow, she suddenly took him by the hand and drew him aside to a quiet turret-chamber flooded with moonlight. There she flung herself on his breast, stroked his fair beard, and thanked him for his coming and for his affection. Honest Zendelwald, however, wished to ascertain whether he were dreaming or waking, and questioned her about how matters really stood, especially about his double. For a long time, she did not understand him; but one word led to another. Zendelwald said this and that had happened to him, and told her all about his journey, about his turning in to the little church, and how he had fallen asleep there and been too late for the tournament.

At that the affair became so far clear to Bertrade that she recognized for the second time the hand of her gracious patroness. But now at last she had opportunity to regard the valiant knight boldly as a gift from Heaven, and she was grateful enough to press the substantial present to her heart in good earnest and return him full measure for the luscious kiss which she had received from Heaven itself.

But, from that time forth, Sir Zendelwald lost all his sluggishness and dreamy irresolution. He said everything and did everything at the right time before the tender Bertrade and before the rest of the world, and he became a great man in the Empire, so that the Emperor was as well content with him as was his wife.

As for Zendelwald's mother, she appeared at the wedding mounted on horseback, and as proud as if she had been enthroned in fortune all her life long. She looked after money and estates, and hunted in the extensive forests to an advanced age. Bertrade never failed to have Zendelwald take her once a year to the lonely little castle which was his home, where she cooed in the grey tower with her darling as tenderly as the wild doves in the trees round about. But they never omitted to enter the little church on their way, and address their prayers to the Virgin, who stood there as prim and saintly as if she had never once come down from her altar.

THE VIRGIN AND THE NUN

O that I had wings like a dove: for then would I flee away, and be at rest. Psalm lv. 6.

A convent lay on a mountain overlooking a wide prospect, and its walls gleamed across the land. Within, it was full of women, beautiful and unbeautiful, who all served the Lord and his Virgin Mother after a strict rule.

The most beautiful of the nuns was called Beatrix, and was sacristan of the convent. Of tall and commanding presence, she went about her duties with stately carriage, saw to choir and altar, looked after the sacristy, and rang the bell before the first flush of dawn and when the evening-star arose.

Yet amid it all she cast many a tear-dimmed glance at the busy loom of the blue distance. There she saw weapons glancing, heard the horn of the hunters in the woods, and the clear shout of men, and her breast filled with longing for the world.

At last she could control her desire no longer, and one clear, moonlit night in June she rose, dressed herself, and put on stout new shoes, and went to the altar, equipped for a journey. "I have served thee faithfully these many years," she said to the Virgin Mary, "but now take the keys thyself; for I can endure the heat in my heart no longer!" With that she laid her bundle of keys upon the altar, and went forth from the convent. She made her way down amid the solitude of the mountain, and wandered on until she came to a cross-road in an oak-forest, where, uncertain which way to take, she sat down by the side of a spring, which was provided with a stone basin and a bench for the benefit of wayfarers. Until the sun rose, she sat there, and was drenched with the falling dew.

33

Then the sun came over the tops of the trees, and the first rays which shot through the forest-road fell on a glittering knight who came riding in full armour all alone. The nun stared with all her lovely eyes, and did not lose an inch of the manly apparition; but she kept so still that the knight would never have seen her had not the murmur of the fountain caught his ear and guided his eyes. He at once turned aside to the spring, dismounted from his horse and let it drink, while he greeted the nun respectfully. He was a crusader who, after long absence, was making his way home alone, for he had lost all his men.

In spite of his respectfulness, he never once removed his eyes from the charms of Beatrix, who held hers just as steady, and gazed as fixedly as ever on the warrior; for he was no inconsiderable part of that world for which she had longed so in secret. But suddenly she cast down her eyes and felt bashful. At last the knight asked her which way she was going, and whether he could be of any service to her. The full tones of his voice startled her; she looked at him once more, and, fascinated by his glances, acknowledged that she had run away from the convent to see the world, but that she was frightened already and did not know which way to turn.

At that the knight, who had all his wits about him, laughed heartily, and offered to conduct the lady so far on the right way, if she would trust herself to him. His castle, he added, was not more than a day's journey from where they were; and there, if she chose, she could make her preparations in security, and after more mature reflection could proceed on her way into the fair, wide world.

Without replying, but yet without opposition, she allowed herself, trembling somewhat nevertheless, to be lifted up on horseback. The knight swung himself up after her, and, with the rosy-blushing nun before him, trotted joyously through woods and meadows.

For two or three hundred lengths, she held herself erect and gazed straight before her, her hands clasped over her bosom. But soon she had laid her head back on his breast, and submitted to the kisses which the stalwart lord imprinted thereon. And by another three hundred lengths she was returning them as fervidly as if she had never rung a convent-bell. In such circumstances, they saw nothing of the bright landscape through which they journeyed. The nun, who once had longed to see the wide world, now shut her eyes to it, and confined herself to that portion of it which the horse could carry on its back.

The knight Wonnebold also scarcely gave a thought to his father's castle, until its towers glittered before him in the moonlight. But all was silent without the castle, and even more silent within, while never a light was to be seen. Wonnebold's father and mother were dead and all the menials departed, save an ancient castellan, who after long knocking made his appearance with a lantern, and almost died for joy when he saw the knight standing at the painfully-opened door. In spite of his solitude and his years the old man had maintained the interior of the castle in habitable condition, and especially had kept the knight's chamber in constant readiness, so that he might be able to go to rest the moment he should return from his travels. So Beatrix rested with him and appeased her longing.

Neither had any thought now of separating from the other. Wonnebold opened his mother's chests. Beatrix clad herself in her rich garments and adorned herself with her jewels, and so they lived for the moment splendidly and in joy, except that the lady remained without rights or title, and was regarded by her lover as his chattel; she desired nothing better for the mean time.

But one day a stranger baron and his train turned into the castle, which by this time was again staffed with servants, and great cheer was made in his honour. At length the men fell to dicing, at which the master of the house had such constant good luck that, flushed with good fortune and confidence, he risked his dearest possession, as he called it, to wit the fair Beatrix as she stood, with the costly jewels she was wearing, against an old, melancholy mountain-keep which his opponent laughingly staked.

Beatrix, who had looked on at the game well contented, now turned pale, and with good reason; for the throw which ensued left the presumptuous one in the lurch, and made the baron the winner.

He wasted no time, but at once took his leave with his fair prize and his attendants. Beatrix barely found time to appropriate the unlucky dice and hide them in her bosom, and then with streaming tears followed the unfeeling winner.

After the little cavalcade had ridden some miles they reached a pleasant grove of young beeches, through which a clear brook flowed. Like a light-green silken tent, the tender foliage waved aloft, supported on the slender silvery stems, between which the spacious summer landscape was seen in glimpses. Here the baron meant to rest with his booty. He ordered his people to go a little farther ahead, while he got down in the pleasant greenwood with Beatrix, and made to draw her to his side with caresses.

At that she drew herself up proudly, and darting a flaming glance upon him exclaimed that he had won her person, but not her heart, which was not to be won against an old ruin. If he were a man, he would set something worth while against it. If he would stake his life, he might cast for her heart, which should be pledged to him for ever and be his own if he won; but if she won, his life should be in her hand, and she should be absolute mistress of her own person once again.

She said this with great gravity; but all the time looked at him with such a strange expression that his heart began to thump, and he regarded her in bewilderment. She seemed to become more and more beautiful as she continued in a softer voice, and with a searching look, "Who would choose to woo a woman when she returns not his wooing, and has received no proof of his courage? Give me your sword, take these dice, and risk it; then we may be united as two true lovers!" At the same time she pressed into his hand the ivory dice warm from her bosom. Bewitched, he gave her his sword and sword-belt, and forthwith threw eleven at one throw.

Next Beatrix took the dice, rattled them vigorously in her hollowed hands with a secret sigh to the Holy Mary the Mother of God, and threw twelve, so that she won.

"I make you a present of your life!" she said, bowed gravely to the baron, picked up her skirts and put the sword under her arm, and rapidly took her departure in the direction whence she had come. As soon as she was out of view of the still quite nonplussed and bewildered baron, she slyly proceeded no farther, but fetched a circuit about the grove, walked quietly back into it, and hid herself not fifty paces from the disappointed lover behind the beech-stems, which at that distance grew sufficiently closely to hide the prudent lady, if need were. She kept quite still; only a sunbeam fell upon a noble gem at her neck, so that it flashed through the grove unknown to her. The baron indeed saw the gleam, and stared at it a moment in his bewilderment. But he took it for a shining dewdrop on a tree-leaf, and never gave it a second thought.

At last he recovered from his stupefaction, and blew lustily upon his hunting-horn. When his people came, he sprang upon his horse, and pursued after the eloping lady to secure her again. It was the best part of an hour before the riders returned, and despondently and slowly made their way through the beech-trees, this time without halting. When the lurking Beatrix saw the coast clear, she rose and hastened home without sparing her shoes.

During all this time Wonnebold had passed a very bad day, racked by remorse and anger; and, as he understood that he had disgraced himself in the eyes of his love, whom he had gambled away so lightly, he began to realize how highly he had unconsciously esteemed her, and how difficult it was to live without her. So, when she unexpectedly stood before him, without ever waiting to utter his surprise, he opened his arms to her, and she hastened into them without complaint or reproach. He laughed loudly as she related her stratagem, and he began to ponder over her fidelity; for the baron was a very comely and pretty fellow.

Accordingly, to guard against all future mischances, he made the fair Beatrix his lawful wedded wife in presence of all his peers and vassals, so that henceforth she ranked as a knight's lady and took her place among her equals at chase, feast and dance, as well as in the cottages of their dependents and in the family seat at church.

The years passed with their changes, and in the course of twelve fruitful harvests she bore her husband eight sons, who grew up like young stags.

When the eldest was eighteen years old, she rose one autumn night from her Wonnebold's side unperceived by him, laid all her worldly array carefully in the same chests from which it had once been taken, closed them, and laid the keys at the sleeper's side. Then she went barefooted to the bedside of her sons, and kissed them lightly one after the other. Last of all, she went again to her husband's bed, kissed him too, and then shore the long hair from her head, once more put on the dark nun's frock, which she had preserved carefully, and so left the castle by stealth, and made her way amid the raging wind of the autumn night and the falling leaves back to that convent from which she had once run away. Indefatigably she passed the beads of her rosary through her fingers, and as she prayed she thought over the life which she had enjoyed.

So she went on her pilgrimage uncomplaining, until she stood again before the convent-door. When she knocked, the door-keeper, who had aged somewhat, opened and greeted her by name as indifferently as if she had only been absent half an hour. Beatrix went past her into the church, and fell on her knees before the altar of the Holy Virgin, who began to speak and said, "Thou hast stayed away rather long, my daughter. I have seen to thy duties as sacristan all the time; but now I am very glad that thou art returned and canst take back thy keys!"

The image leaned down, and handed the keys to Beatrix, who was both alarmed and delighted at the great miracle. Forthwith she set about her duties, saw to this and that, and when the bell rang for dinner she went to table. Many of the nuns had grown old, others were dead, young ones were newly come, and another abbess sat at the head of the table; but no one suspected what had happened to Beatrix, who took her accustomed seat; for Mary had filled her place in the nun's own form.

But another day, when some ten years had passed, the nuns were to celebrate a great festival, and agreed that each of them should bring the Mother of God the finest present she could devise. So one embroidered a rich church-banner, another an altar-cloth, and another a vestment. One composed a Latin hymn, and another set it to music. A third wrote and illuminated a prayer-book. Whoever could do nothing else stitched a new shirt for the Christ-child, and sister cook made him a dish of fritters. Only Beatrix had prepared nothing, for she was rather weary of life, and she lived with her thoughts more in the past than in the present.

When the feast-day came, and she had no gift to dedicate, the other nuns were surprised and reproached her so that she sat humbly aside as all the pretty things

37

were being borne in festal procession and laid before the altar of the church, which was adorned with flowers, while the bells rang out and the incense-clouds rose on high.

Just as the nuns were proceeding to sing and play right skilfully, a grey-headed knight passed by on his way, with eight armed youths as lovely as pictures, all mounted on proud steeds and attended by a like number of tall squires. It was Wonnebold with his sons, whom he was taking to the Imperial army.

Perceiving that high Mass was being celebrated in God's house, he called to his sons to dismount, and entered the church with them to offer a devout prayer to the Holy Virgin. Every one was lost in admiration at the noble spectacle, as the iron greybeard knelt with the eight youthful warriors, who looked like so many mail-clad angels; and the nuns were so put off their music that for a moment it ceased altogether. But Beatrix recognized them all for her children, from her husband, gave an exclamation and hastened to them, and, recalling herself to their memory, disclosed her secret, and declared the great miracle which she had experienced.

Then all were forced to admit that she had brought the Virgin the richest gift of the day. That it was accepted was testified by eight wreaths of fresh oak-leaves which suddenly appeared on the young men's heads, placed there by the invisible hand of the Queen of Heaven.

THE NAUGHTY SAINT VITALIS

Be not familiar with any woman: but in general commend all good women to God.

Thomas à Kempis, *Imitatio* i. 8.

At the beginning of the eighth century there lived in Alexandria of Egypt an extraordinary monk, by name Vitalis, who had made it his particular task to reclaim the souls of lost women from the ways of sin and lead them back to virtue. But the method which he pursued was so peculiar, and the fondness, nay enthusiasm, with which he unceasingly prosecuted his ends, was alloyed with such remarkable self-abasement and simulation, that the like was scarcely ever known in the world.

He kept an exact roll of all those wantons on a neat slip of parchment, and, whenever he discovered a new quarry in the city or its environs, he immediately noted her name and dwelling on it; so that the naughty young patricians of Alexandria could have found no better guide than the industrious Vitalis, had he been disposed to harbour less saintly aims. As it was, the monk wormed out much news and information for his business from his sly and frivolous conversations with them; but he never suffered the scamps to pick up any information of the sort from him.

He carried this directory in his cowl, rolled up in a silver case, and drew it out repeatedly to add a newly-discovered light name, or to run over those already inscribed, count them, and reckon which of the occupants should have her turn next.

Then he would seek her hurriedly and half ashamed, and say hastily, "Keep the night after to-morrow for me, and promise no one else!" When he entered the house at the appointed time, he would leave the fair one standing, and betake him to the farthest corner of the room, fall on his knees, and pray fervently and at the pitch of his voice all night long for the occupant of the house. In the early morning he would leave her, and charge her strictly not to tell any one what had passed between them.

So he went on for a good while, and got himself into very ill odour indeed. For while in secret, behind the closed doors of the wantons, he alarmed and touched many a lost woman by his fiery words of thunder and the fervent sweetness of his murmured prayers, so that she came to herself and began to lead a holy life; in the public eye, on the contrary, he appeared to have laid himself out of set purpose to merit the reputation of a vicious and sinful monk, who wallowed gleefully in all the debaucheries of the world, and flaunted his religious habit as a banner of shame.

If he found himself of an evening at dusk in respectable company, he would exclaim abruptly, "Oh! what am I about? I had almost forgotten that the brunette Doris is waiting for me, the little dear! The deuce! I must be off, or she will be vexed!"

If any one reproached him, he would cry out as if incensed, "Do you think that I am a stone? Do you imagine that God did not create a little woman for a monk?" If any one said, "Father, you would be better to lay aside your frock and marry, so as not to offend others," he would answer, "Let them be offended if they choose, and run their heads against a wall! Who is my judge?"

All this he used to say with great vehemence and all the address of an actor, like one who defends a bad cause with a multitude of bold words.

And he would go off and quarrel with the other suitors before the girls' doors. He would even come to blows with them, and administered many a rude buffet when they said, "Away with the monk! Does the cleric mean to dispute the ground with us? Get out, bald-pate!"

But he was so obstinate and persistent that in most cases he got the better of them, and slipped into the house before they knew where they were.

When he returned to his cell in the grey of the morning, he would cast himself down before the Mother of God, to whose sole honour and praise he undertook those adventures and drew down on himself the world's blame; and, did he succeed in bringing back some lost lamb and placing her in some holy convent, he felt more blissful in the presence of Heaven's Queen than if he had converted a thousand heathen. For this was his very remarkable taste, to endure the martyrdom of appearing in the eye of the world as an unclean profligate, while all the time Our Undefiled Lady in Heaven was well aware that he had never touched a woman, and that he wore an invisible crown of white roses on his much-maligned head.

Once he heard of a peculiarly dangerous person, who by her beauty and unusual charms had occasioned much trouble, and even bloodshed, inasmuch as a ferocious military dandy laid siege to her door, and struck down all who attempted to dispute her possession with him. Vitalis immediately proposed the attack and conquest of this hell. He did not wait to write the fair sinner's name in his list, but went straight off to the notorious house, and at the door, sure enough, encountered the soldier, who was stalking along, clad in scarlet, and with a javelin in his hand.

"Dodge aside, monkling!" he shouted contemptuously to the pious Vitalis. "How dare you come sneaking about my lion's den? Heaven is your place; the world is ours!"

"Heaven and earth and all that therein is," said Vitalis, "belong to the Lord, and to his merry servants! Pack! you gaudy lout, and let me go where I choose."

The warrior wrathfully raised the shaft of his javelin to bring it down on the monk's pate; but he suddenly pulled out a peaceful olive-branch from beneath his frock, parried the blow, and smote the bully so roughly on the crown that he wellnigh lost his senses, after which the fighting cleric gave him several raps on the muzzle, until the soldier, completely dumbfounded, made off cursing.

Thereupon Vitalis forced his way triumphantly into the house, where, at the head of a narrow staircase, the woman stood with a light in her hand, listening to the noise and shouting. She was an uncommonly fine figure of a woman, with beautiful, strong but rather defiant, features, about which her reddish hair floated in abundant loose waves, like a lion's mane.

She looked down contemptuously on Vitalis as he ascended, and said, "Where are you going?" "To you, my dove!" he answered. "Have you never heard of the tender monk Vitalis, the jolly Vitalis?" But she answered harshly, as she blocked the staircase with her powerful figure, "Have you money, monk?" Disconcerted, he said, "Monks do not carry money about with them." "Then trot off," she said, "or I'll have you beaten out of the house with firebrands!"

Vitalis scratched his head, completely nonplussed, for he had never reckoned on this happening. The creatures whom he had hitherto converted had naturally thought no more of the price of iniquity, and those whom he failed to convert contented themselves with hard words in compensation for the precious time which he had made them lose. But here he could get no footing inside to begin his pious work; and yet there was something hugely attractive in the prospect of breaking in this red-haired daughter of Satan; for large and beautiful figures of men and women always mislead the judgement, so that we attribute greater qualities to them than they really possess. In desperation he searched through his frock, and came upon the silver case, which was adorned with an amethyst of some value. "I have nothing but this," he said; "let me in for it!" She took the case, examined it carefully, then bade him come with her. Arrived at her bedchamber, he did not favour her with another glance; but knelt down in a corner after his custom, and began to pray aloud.

The harlot, who believed that from force of habit the holy man meant to begin his worldly performance with prayer, broke into uncontrollable laughter, and sat down on her couch to look at him, for his behaviour amused her monstrously. But as the business never came to an end, and was beginning to weary her, she bared her shoulders immodestly, went up to him, clasped him in her strong, white arms, and pressed the good Vitalis with his shorn and tonsured head so roughly against her breast that he was like to choke, and began to gasp as if the flames of purgatory had taken hold of him. But it did not last long; he began to kick out in all directions like a young horse in a smithy, until he freed himself from the hellish embrace. Then he took the long cord which he wore about his waist, and caught hold of the woman, to bind her hands behind her back, and have peace from her. He had to wrestle hard with her before he succeeded in tying her up. He bound her feet together as well, and threw the whole bundle with a mighty heave upon the bed; after which he betook himself to his corner again, and continued his prayers as if nothing had happened.

The captive lioness at first turned about angrily and restlessly, endeavouring to release herself, and uttered a hundred curses. Then she became quieter as the monk never ceased to pray, to preach, to adjure her, and towards morning she uttered manifest sighs, which, as it seemed, were soon followed by contrite sobbing. In short, when the sun rose, she was lying like a Magdalene at his feet, released from her bonds, and bedewing the hem of his garment with tears. With dignity, yet with gladness, Vitalis stroked her head, and promised to pay her

41

another visit as soon as it was dark, to inform her in what convent he had found a penitent's cell for her. Then he left, not forgetting first to impress upon her that she was to say nothing in the meantime about her conversion, but only tell any one who might enquire, that he had been very merry with her.

But judge of his surprise, when he reappeared at the appointed time, and found the door shut fast, and the female freshly bedizened in all her glory looking out of the window.

"What do you want, priest?" she cried down. And in astonishment he answered in an undertone, "What does this mean, my lamb? Put away those sinful baubles, and let me in to prepare you for your penance." "You want in to me, you naughty monk?" she said with a smile, as if she had misunderstood him. "Have you money, or money's worth, about you?" Vitalis stared up open-mouthed, then shook the door desperately; but it remained shut as fast as ever, and the woman too disappeared from the window.

At last the laughter and imprecations of the passersby drove the apparently depraved and shameless monk away from the door of the house of ill fame. But his thought and endeavour ran entirely upon making his way into the house again, and finding some means or other to overcome the devil by which the woman was possessed.

Absorbed in such thoughts, he turned his steps to a church, where, instead of praying, he thought over ways and means by which he might contrive to gain access to the lost woman. While thus engaged, his eye fell upon the box in which the charitable offerings were kept, and scarcely was the church deserted (it had become dark), when he burst the box violently open with his fist, poured the contents, which consisted of a lot of small silver coins, into his tucked-up frock, and hastened faster than any lover to the sinful woman's abode.

A foppish admirer was about to slip in at the opening door. Vitalis seized him from behind by his perfumed locks, flung him into the street, slammed the door in his face as he sprang in himself, and in another instant found himself once again in the presence of the disreputable person, who glared at him with flaming eyes when he appeared instead of her expected admirer. But Vitalis promptly poured the stolen money out on the table, saying, "Is that enough for to-night?" Without a word, but carefully, she counted the sum, said "It is enough!" and put it away.

Now they confronted each other in the strangest fashion. Biting her lips to restrain a laugh, she looked at him with a simulated air of utter ignorance; while the monk scrutinized her with undecided and anxious glances, not knowing how he should begin to bring her to book. But when she suddenly proceeded to alluring gestures, and made to stroke his dark, glossy beard, the storm of his saintly character broke out in all its fury, he struck her hand indignantly away,

42

and flung her upon the couch so that it shook. Then kneeling upon her, and grasping her hands, unaffected by her charms, he began to speak home to her in such fashion that at last her obduracy seemed to soften.

She desisted from her violent struggles to free herself. Copious tears flowed over her strong and lovely features, and, when at length the zealous man of God released her, and stood erect beside her sinful couch, the great form lay upon it with weary, relaxed limbs, as if broken by repentance and remorse, sobbing and turning her tear-dimmed eyes upon him, as if in astonishment at her unwilling transformation.

Then the tempest of his eloquent wrath changed likewise to tender emotion and deep sympathy. In his heart he gave praise to his Heavenly protectress, in whose honour this hardest of all his victories had been gained; and now his words of forgiveness and consolation flowed like the mild breath of spring over the broken ice of her heart.

More delighted than if he had enjoyed the sweetest favours of love, he hastened thence, not to snatch a brief slumber on his hard bed, but to throw himself down before the Virgin's altar, and pray for the poor repentant soul until the day had fully dawned. Then he vowed not to close an eye until the strayed lamb was finally safe within the shelter of the convent-walls.

The morning was scarcely astir when he was again on the way to her house. But he saw approaching at the same moment from the other end of the street the fierce warrior, who, after a riotous night, had taken it into his half-drunken head to wind up with a fresh conquest of the harlot.

Vitalis was the nearer to the unhallowed door, and he sprang nimbly forward to reach it. Thereupon the other hurled his spear at him, which buried itself just beside the monk's head in the door so that its shaft quivered. But, before it had ceased quivering, the monk wrenched it out of the wood with all his force, faced the infuriated soldier as he sprang towards him brandishing a naked sword, and quick as lightning drove the spear through his breast. The man sank in a heap, dead, and Vitalis was almost instantly seized and bound by a troop of soldiers, who were returning from the night-watch and had seen his deed, and he was led away to gaol.

In genuine anguish he looked back to the house, where he could no longer accomplish his good work. The watch thought that he was simply deploring his evil star which had baulked him of his wicked purpose, and treated the apparently incorrigible monk to blows and hard words until he was safely in ward.

He had to lie there for many days, and was several times brought before the judge. True, he was at length discharged without punishment, seeing that he had killed the man in self-defence. But nevertheless he came out of the affair with the reputation of a homicide, and every one cried out that now, surely, they must unfrock him. But Bishop Joannes, who was then chief at Alexandria, must have had some inkling of the real state of affairs, or else have cherished some deeper design; for he declined to expel the disreputable monk from the clergy, and ordered that for the present he was to be allowed to continue his extraordinary career.

He lost no time in returning to the converted sinner, who in the interval had gone back to her old ways, and would not admit the horrified and distressed Vitalis until he had appropriated another object of value and brought it to her. She repented and converted a third, and likewise a fourth and fifth time, for she found these conversions more lucrative than anything else, and moreover the evil spirit in her found an infernal satisfaction in mocking the poor monk with an endless variety of devices and inventions.

As for him, he now became a veritable martyr inwardly and outwardly; for, the more cruelly he was deceived, the more he felt compelled to exert himself, and it seemed to him as if his own eternal welfare depended on the reformation of this one person. He was already a homicide, a violator of churches, a thief; but he would rather have cut off his hand than part with the least portion of his reputation as a profligate; and, though all this became harder and harder for his heart to bear, he strove all the more eagerly to maintain his wicked exterior in the world's eye by means of frivolous speech. For this was the special form of martyrdom which he had elected. All the same, he became pale and thin, and began to flit about like a shadow on the wall, though always with a laughing face.

Now over against that house of torment dwelt a rich Greek merchant who had an only daughter called Iole, who could do what she liked, and consequently never knew what to do with herself all the live-long day. For her father, who was retired from business, studied Plato, and when tired of him he would compose neat epigrams on the ancient engraved gems of which he had a large collection; but Iole, when she had laid aside her music, could think of no outlet for her lively fancies, and would peep out restlessly at the sky and at the distance, from every peep-hole she found.

So it came about that she discovered the monk's coming and going in the street, and ascertained how matters stood with the notorious cleric. Startled and shy, she peeped at him from her safe concealment, and could not help commiserating his handsome form and manly appearance. When she learned from one of her maids, who was intimate with a maid of the wicked strumpet, how Vitalis was being deceived by her, and what was the real truth about him, she was amazed beyond measure, and, far from respecting his martyrdom, was overcome by a strange indignation, and considered this sort of holiness little conducive to the honour of her sex. She dreamed and puzzled over it a while, and became always the more displeased, while, at the same time, her partiality for the monk increased and conflicted with her wrath.

All of a sudden she resolved that if the Virgin Mary had not sense enough to lead the erring monk back to more respectable ways, she would undertake the task herself, and lend the Virgin a hand in the business, little dreaming that she was the unwitting instrument of the Queen of Heaven, who had now begun to intervene. Forthwith she went to her father, and complained bitterly to him of the unseemly proximity of the lady of pleasure, and adjured him to employ his wealth in getting her out of the way immediately, at any price.

In obedience to her directions, the old gentleman addressed himself to the person, and offered her a certain sum for her house, on condition that she handed it over at once, and left the neighbourhood entirely. She desired nothing better; and that same forenoon she had disappeared from the quarter, while the old merchant was sitting once more over his Plato and had dismissed the whole affair from his mind.

Not so Iole, who was in the utmost eagerness to rid the house from top to bottom of every trace of its former occupant. When it was all swept and garnished, she had it fumigated with rare spices so that the fragrant clouds poured out from all the windows.

Then she furnished the empty room with nothing but a carpet, a rose-bush, and a lamp, and, as soon as her father, who went to bed with the sun, was asleep, she went across, with a wreath of roses adorning her hair, and took her seat alone on the outspread carpet, while two trusty old servants kept watch at the door.

They turned away several night-revellers, but, whenever they saw Vitalis approach, they hid themselves and allowed him to pass in unhindered by the open door. With many sighs, he climbed the stair, full of fear lest he should see himself made a fool of once again, full of hope that he might be freed at last from this burden by the genuine repentance of a creature who was hindering him from rescuing so many other souls. But judge of his astonishment, when he entered the room, and found it stripped of all the wild red lioness's trumpery, and instead of her a sweet and tender form sitting on the carpet with the rose-bush opposite her on the floor.

"Where is the wretched creature, who used to live here?" he exclaimed, looking about him in wonder, and finally letting his eyes rest on the lovely apparition which he saw before him.

"She has gone out into the Desert," answered Iole, without looking up. "There she means to live as an anchorite and do penance. It came upon her suddenly

45

this morning, and broke her like a straw, and her conscience is awakened at last. She cried out for a certain priest Vitalis, who could have helped her. But the spirit which had entered into her would not suffer her to wait. The fool gathered all her possessions together, sold them, and gave the money to the poor, then went off hot-foot with a hair-cloth shift, and shorn hair, and a staff in her hand, the way of the Desert."

"Glory to thee, O Lord, and praise to thy Gracious Mother!" cried Vitalis, his hands folded in glad devotion, while a burden as of stone fell from his heart. But at the same time he looked more narrowly at the maiden with her rose-wreath, and said, "Why do you call her a fool? and who are you? and where do you come from? and what are you about?"

At that the lovely Iole cast her dark eyes to the ground lower than ever. She hung her head, and a bright flush of modesty spread over her face, for she thought shame of herself for the sad things she was going to say before a man.

"I am an outcast orphan, who have neither father nor mother. This lamp and carpet and rose-bush are the last remnants of my inheritance, and I have settled in this house with them to take up the life which my predecessor here has abandoned."

"Ah, so you would--!" the monk exclaimed, and clapped his hands. "Just see how busy the Devil is! And this innocent creature says the thing as indifferently as if I were not Vitalis! Now my kitten, how do you mean to do? Just tell me!"

"I mean to devote myself to love and serve the men as long as this rose lives!" she said, pointing hastily at the flower-pot. Still, she could hardly get the words out, and almost sank on the floor for shame, so deeply did she droop her head. This natural modesty served the little rogue well; for it convinced the monk that he had to do this time with a childish innocent, who was possessed by the Devil and was on the point of jumping plump into the abyss. He caressed his beard in satisfaction at having arrived on the scene so opportunely for once, and, to enjoy his satisfaction still longer, he said slowly and jestingly, "Then afterwards, my dove?"

"Afterwards I will go, a poor lost soul, to Hell where beauteous Dame Venus is; or perhaps, if I meet a good preacher, I may even enter a convent later on, and do penance!"

"Better and better!" he cried. "That is an orderly plan of campaign, indeed, and not badly thought out. For, so far as the preacher is concerned, he is here now, he is standing before you, you black-eyed Devil's tit-bit! And the convent is all ready rigged up for you, like a mousetrap, only you'll go into it without having sinned, do you see? Without having sinned in anything but the pretty intention, which after all may make a very toothsome bone of repentance for you to gnaw all your days, and may serve your turn. For without it, you little witch, you would be too comical and light-hearted for a real penitent! But now!" he continued seriously, "first off with the roses, and then listen attentively!"

"No!" answered Iole, somewhat more pertly. "I will listen first, and then see whether I'll take off the roses. Now that I have once overcome my womanly feelings, mere words will not suffice to restrain me until I know the sin. And, without sin, I can know nothing about repentance. I give you this to think over before you begin your efforts. But still I am willing to hear you."

Then Vitalis began the finest exhortation he had ever delivered. The maiden listened good-naturedly and attentively, and the sight of her had, unknown to him, a considerable influence on his choice of language; for the beauty and daintiness of the prospective convert were themselves enough to evoke a lofty eloquence. But, as she was not the least bit in earnest about the project which she had so outrageously advertised, the monk's oration could not have any very serious effect upon her. On the contrary, a charming laugh flitted about her mouth, and, when he had concluded, and expectantly wiped the sweat from his brow, Iole said, "I am only half moved by your words, and cannot decide to give up my project; for I am only too curious to know what it is like to live in sin and pleasure!"

Vitalis stood as if petrified, and could not get so much as one word out. It was the first time that his powers of conversion had failed so roundly. Sighing and thoughtful, he paced up and down the room, and took another look at the little candidate for Hell. The power of the Devil seemed to have combined in some bewildering fashion with the power of innocence to thwart him. But he was all the more passionately anxious to overcome them.

"I do not leave this place until you repent," he cried at length, "not though I should spend three days and three nights here!"

"That would only make me more obstinate," responded Iole. "But I will take time to think, and will hear you again to-morrow night. The day will soon be dawning now. Go your way. Meantime I promise to do nothing in the matter, and to remain in my present condition; in return for which you must promise on no account to mention me to anybody, and to come here only under cover of darkness."

"So be it!" exclaimed Vitalis, and took his departure, while Iole slipped quickly back into her father's house.

She did not sleep long, and awaited the coming evening with impatience. For the monk, now that he had been so close to her throughout the night, pleased her better than he had done at a distance. She saw now what a fire of enthusiasm glowed in his eyes, and how resolute all his movements were, despite his

47

monkish garments. And when she represented to herself his self-abnegation, his perseverance in the course he had once chosen, she could not help wishing that those good qualities were utilized to her own pleasure and profit, in the shape of a cherished and faithful husband. Her project, accordingly, was to make a brave martyr into a still better husband.

The next night she found Vitalis at her carpet in good time, and he continued his exertions on behalf of her virtue with undiminished zeal. He had to stand all the time, except when he knelt to pray. Iole, on the contrary, made herself comfortable. She laid herself back on the carpet, clasped her hands behind her head, and kept her half-closed eyes steadily fixed upon the monk as he stood and preached. Sometimes she closed them as if overcome by drowsiness, and, as soon as Vitalis saw this, he pushed her with his foot to waken her. But this harsh measure always turned out milder than he intended; for, as soon as his foot neared the maiden's slender side, it spontaneously moderated its force, and touched her tender ribs quite gently; not to mention that a most unusual sensation ran along the whole length of the monk, a sensation which he had never before experienced in the slightest degree from any of the numerous fair sinners with whom he had had to deal.

As morning approached, Iole nodded more and more frequently, till at last Vitalis exclaimed indignantly, "Child, you are not listening! I can't keep you awake. You are utterly sunk in sloth!"

"Not so!" she said, as she suddenly opened her eyes, and a sweet smile flitted across her face, as if the approaching day were already reflected in it. "I have been paying attention; I am beginning to hate that wretched sin, which is all the more repulsive to me that it causes you vexation, dear monk; for nothing could be pleasing to me that is displeasing to you."

"Really?" he queried, full of joy. "So I have really succeeded? Come away to the convent at once, that we may make sure of you. This time we'll strike while the iron's hot."

"You do not understand me aright," Iole answered, and, blushing, cast her eyes again to the ground. "I am enamoured of you, and have conceived a tender inclination towards you!"

For a moment, Vitalis felt as if a hand had smitten his heart; yet he did not feel that it caused him pain. Paralysed, he opened wide his mouth and eyes, and stood stock-still.

But Iole, blushing redder than ever, went on to say gently and softly, "You must now lecture me and charm away this new mischief from me, in order to deliver me entirely from the malady, and I hope you may succeed!"

Vitalis, without saying a word, turned tail and ran out of the house. Instead of seeking his bed, he rushed out into the silvery grey morning, and debated whether he should leave this dangerous young woman to her fate and have done with her, or should endeavour to cast out this latest whim also, which appeared to be the most reprehensible of all her notions, and not altogether without danger to himself. But a wrathful flush of shame flew to his head at the thought that anything of the sort could be perilous for him. Then again it occurred to him that the Devil might have set a snare for him, in which case it were best to avoid it betimes. But to become a deserter in the face of such a wisp of a temptress! And supposing the poor creature were in earnest, and could be cured of her latest unseemly delusion by a few rough words? In short, Vitalis could not settle within himself, all the more that at the bottom of his heart a dim wave was beginning to cause the skiff of his reason to be unsteady.

In his perplexity he slipped into a little chapel where a beautiful ancient marble statue of the goddess Juno had recently been set up with a golden nimbus as an image of the Virgin Mary, so as not to waste such a gift of divine art. He cast himself down before this Mary, and laid his doubts fervently before her, and prayed his patroness for a token. If she nodded, he would complete Iole's conversion; if she shook her head, he would desist.

But the image left him in the most cruel uncertainty, and did neither one thing nor the other; it neither nodded nor shook its head. Only when the red gleam of some flying morning clouds passed over the marble, its face seemed to smile most propitiously; whether it was that the ancient goddess, as guardian deity of connubial love and chastity, was giving a sign, or that the new one could not refrain from smiling at her adorer's troubles; for both were women at heart, and such are always tickled when a love-affair is in train. But Vitalis knew nothing of all this. On the contrary, the beauty of the expression raised his courage amazingly, and, still more remarkable to relate, the statue appeared to assume the features of the blushing Iole, who was challenging him to expel her love of him from her mind.

Meantime, at the same hour, Iole's father was strolling beneath the cypresses of his garden. He had acquired some very fine new gems, the engraving on which had brought him out of bed at that early hour. He was handling them rapturously, and making them play in the beams of the rising sun. There was a dark amethyst, on which Luna drove her car through the heavens, unwitting that Love was squatted behind her, while flying Cupids called to her the Greek for "Whip behind!" A handsome onyx showed Minerva lost in meditation, holding Love on her knee, who was busy polishing her breast-plate with his hand to see his own reflection.

And lastly, on a cornelian, Love, in the form of a salamander, was tumbling about in a vestal fire and throwing its guardian virgins into perplexity and alarm.

These scenes tempted the old man to compose some distichs, and he was considering which he should attack first when his daughter Iole came through the garden, pale and unslept. Anxious and surprised, he called her to him and enquired what had robbed her of her slumbers. But, before she could answer, he began to show her his gems and explain them to her.

At that she heaved a deep sigh and said, "Ah, if all those great powers, Chastity herself, Wisdom, and Religion, could not defend themselves against Love, how is a poor insignificant creature like me to fortify herself against him?"

The old gentleman was not a little astonished at these words. "What do I hear?" he said. "Is it that the dart of mighty Eros has smitten thee?"

"It has pierced me to the heart," she responded, "and, if I am not in possession of the man whom I love within a day and a night, I shall be the bride of Death!"

Although her father was accustomed to let her have her own way in everything she desired, this haste was rather too violent for him, and he recommended repose and reflection to his daughter. But she had no lack of the latter, and she employed it so well that the old man exclaimed, "So I must discharge the most unpleasant of all a father's duties, I must go to your choice, to your man, and lead him by the nose up to the best that I can call mine, and beg him to be so kind as to take possession? Here is a tidy little woman, my dear sir! I pray you, don't despise her! I had much rather give you a box or two on the ear, but my little daughter will die, so I must be civil! So be graciously pleased, for Heaven's sake, to taste the pasty which is offered you. It has been well baked, and will fairly melt in your mouth!"

"All that is spared us," said Iole, "for, if you will only allow me, I hope to bring him to it that he will come himself and ask for my hand."

"And what if this man, whom I know nothing of, turns out to be a wastrel and a good-for-nothing?"

"Then let him be driven away with scorn! But he is a saint!"

"Then run away, and leave me to the Muses," said the good old man.

When evening came, the night did not follow the dusk so promptly as Vitalis appeared at Iole's heels in the familiar house. But he had never entered the house in the same fashion as now. His heart beat, and he was forced to feel what it meant to see again a person who had played such a trump. It was another Vitalis than the one who had descended in the early morning, who now came up the steps, although he himself was the most unconscious of the fact; for the poor converter of frail women and monk of evil renown had never learned the difference between the smile of a harlot and that of an honourable woman.

Yet he came with the best of intentions, and with the old purpose of driving all the idle notions out of the little monster's head for good and all. Only he had a vague idea that once his task was accomplished he might be permitted a pause in his martyr activity; all at once he began to be very tired of it.

But it was determined that some new surprise should always await him in that enchanted dwelling. When he entered the room, he found it beautifully decorated, and furnished with all usual furniture. A delicate, insidious odour of flowers pervaded the room, and was in keeping with a certain modest worldliness. On a snow-white couch, not a fold out of place in its silk coverings, sat Iole, splendidly arrayed, in sweet troubled melancholy, like an angel in meditation. Under the trim pleats of her robe her bosom heaved like the foam on a milking pail, and, though the white arms, which she folded beneath her breast, shone so fair, yet all those charms looked so lawful and permissible in the order of things that Vitalis's accustomed eloquence stuck in his throat.

"You are amazed, my pretty monk," began Iole, "to find all this show and finery here! Know that this is the farewell which I mean to take of the world, and, at the same time, I will lay aside the inclination which, unfortunately, I cannot help feeling for you. But you must help me to this end to the best of your ability, and after the fashion that I have devised and request of you. I mean that when you address me in these garments and as a cleric it is always the same. The bearing of a churchman fails to convince me, for I belong to the world. I cannot be cured of love by a monk, who is unacquainted with love, and does not know what he is talking about. If you really mean to afford me rest and put me on the way to Heaven, go into that closet, where you will find secular clothes laid out ready for you. Exchange your monk's clothes there for them, array yourself like a man of the world, then seat yourself beside me to partake of a little repast with me, and in such worldly externals exert all your acuteness and understanding to wean me from you and incline me to piety."

Vitalis made no reply, but bethought himself a while. Then he decided to end all his difficulties at one stroke, and to put the devil of this world to flight with his own weapons by acceding to Iole's eccentric proposal.

So he actually betook himself into an adjoining closet, where a couple of servants awaited him with splendid garments of purple and fine linen. Scarcely had he put them on, when he looked a good head taller, and it was with a noble mien that he strode back to Iole, who could not take her eyes off him, and clapped her hands for joy.

Now, however, a real miracle and a strange transformation was wrought on the monk. For scarcely had he sat down in his worldly array beside the charming woman, when the immediate past was blown away like a dream from his mind, and he forgot all about his purpose. Instead of speaking so much as a word, he listened eagerly to what was said by Iole, who had taken possession of his hand and begun to tell him her true story, who she was, where she lived, and how it was her most heart-felt desire that he should give over his strange manner of life, and ask her father for her hand, so that he might become a good husband, well-pleasing to God. She also said many wonderful things in the most beautiful words about the history of a happy and chaste love, but concluded with a sigh that she saw well how hopeless her desire was, and that he was now at liberty to argue her out of all those ideas, but not before he had fortified himself duly for his task with meat and drink.

Then at her signal the servants set drinking-vessels on the table together with a basket of cakes and fruits. Iole mixed a goblet of wine for the silent Vitalis, and affectionately handed him something to eat, so that he felt quite at home, and was reminded of his childhood, when as a little boy he was tenderly fed by his mother. He ate and drank, and, when he had done so, it seemed to him as if he might now venture to rest from his long, weary toil, and lo! our Vitalis leant his head to one side, towards Iole, and without more ado fell asleep, and lay till sunrise.

When he awoke, he was alone, and no one was to be seen or heard. He sprang up hastily, and was horrified at the splendid garment in which he was dressed. He rushed madly through the house from top to bottom, seeking for his monk's frock. But not the smallest trace of it could he find, until he chanced to see a little heap of cinders and ashes, on which a sleeve of his priest's dress was lying half consumed, whereupon he rightly concluded that there it had been solemnly burned.

Next he put his head out cautiously, first at one, then at another of the windows which looked on to the street, drawing it in every time that any one approached. At last he flung himself down upon the silken couch as comfortable and at ease as if he had never lain on a monk's hard bed. Then he roused himself, put his dress straight, and stole in high excitement to the street-door. There he still hesitated a moment; but suddenly he flung it wide open, and went out into the world a magnificent and imposing figure. No one recognized him; every one took him for some fine gentleman from abroad, who was enjoying a few gay days at Alexandria.

He looked neither to right nor left, else he would have seen Iole on her house-top. So he went straight back to his convent, where, however, all the monks and their superior had just resolved to expel him from their fellowship; for the measure of his iniquities was now full, and he contributed only to the scandal and disgrace of the Church. The sight of him, actually coming among them in his worldly gallant's attire, knocked the bottom out of the tub of their patience; they drenched him and doused him with water from all sides, and drove him with crosses, besoms, pitchforks and kitchen-ladles out of the convent.

Once on a time this rough handling would have been the height of felicity to him, and a triumph of his martyrdom. True, he laughed inwardly even now, but for a somewhat different reason. He took one more stroll round about the city-walls, and let his red cloak wave in the wind. A fine breeze from the Holy Land blew across the sparkling sea; but Vitalis was becoming more and more worldly-minded. Suddenly he retraced his steps into the bustling streets of the city, sought the house where Iole dwelt, and did what she wished.

He now made as excellent and complete a layman and husband as he had been a martyr. The Church, however, when she understood the real facts of the case, was inconsolable over the loss of such a saint, and made every endeavour to recall the fugitive to her bosom. But Iole held him fast and gave it to be understood that he was in very good hands with her.

DOROTHEA'S FLOWER-BASKET

To lose oneself so is rather to find oneself.
Franciscus Ludovicus Blosius,
Spiritual Instruction, c. 12.

On the south coast of the Euxine sea, not far from the mouth of the river Halys, a Roman country-house lay in the light of the brightest of spring mornings. From the waters of the sea a north-east wind wafted a refreshing coolness through the gardens, as grateful to the pagans and to the secret Christians as it was to the trembling leaves upon the trees.

In a summer-house by the sea-shore, shut off from the rest of the world, stood a young couple, a handsome young man with the daintiest maiden imaginable. She was holding out a large, beautifully-shaped bowl of translucent, warm-hued marble for the youth to admire, and the morning sun shone with great effect through the bowl, so that its ruddy glow concealed the blush on the maiden's visage.

She was Dorothea, a patrician's daughter, to whom Fabricius, governor of the province of Cappadocia, was paying assiduous court. But as he was a bigoted persecutor of the Christians, and Dorothea's parents felt attracted by the new philosophy of life and were making diligent endeavours to adopt it, they were offering the best resistance they could to the powerful inquisitor's importunity. Not that they wished to involve their children in religious controversies, or that they would condescend to barter their hearts for a faith--they were too noble and liberal for that; but they were of opinion that a religious persecutor would never make a good heart's consoler.

Dorothea for her part had no need of such considerations, since she possessed another safeguard against the governor's attentions in the shape of her liking for his private secretary, Theophilus, who was standing beside her at that moment, and looking with interest at the rosy bowl.

Theophilus was an exceedingly refined, cultivated man of Greek descent, who had risen in spite of adverse circumstances and was held in high esteem by all. But the hardships of his early years had left him somewhat suspicious and reserved, and, while he was satisfied with what he owed to his own exertions, he was loth to believe that any one attached himself to him from disinterested motives. The sight of the young Dorothea was dear to him as his life, but the very fact that the chief man in Cappadocia was paying court to her prevented him from cherishing any hopes for himself, and he would not at any price have run the risk of cutting a ridiculous figure beside his lordship.

Nevertheless, Dorothea sought to conduct her desires to a happy issue, and in the meantime to assure herself of his presence as often as possible. Because he always appeared calm and indifferent, her passion provoked her to dangerous little stratagems, and she tried to move him by means of jealousy by pretending to be interested in the governor Fabricius, and to be on friendly terms with him. But poor Theophilus was an innocent in such tricks, and, even if he had understood them, was far too proud to show any jealousy. Yet by degrees he became distracted and perplexed, and sometimes betrayed himself, but always promptly recollected himself and recovered his reserve, so that his tender sweetheart had nothing for it but to proceed somewhat forcibly, and pull in her net unexpectedly when opportunity offered.

He was out in Pontus on state business, and Dorothea, who was aware of this, had accompanied her parents from Cæsarea to the country-house for the spring, which had just begun. Thus she had managed, after painfully-devised and ingenious man[oe]uvres, to get him into the arbour that morning, partly as if by accident, partly as if with friendly intent, so that both his good luck and her good graces should make him happy and confiding, as indeed they did.

She wished to show him the vase, which a kind uncle had sent her as a birthday present from Trebizond. Her countenance was radiant from sheer joy at having her beloved beside her alone, and at being able to show him something pretty, and he too was genuinely happy. Besides, there was sunshine in his heart at last, so that he could no longer keep his lips from smiling trustfully nor his eyes from sparkling.

But the ancients have forgotten to give a name to the envious divinity, the rival of gentle Eros, who, at the critical moment when good fortune is closest at hand, throws a veil over lovers' eyes, and twists the word in their mouth.

As she gave the bowl trustfully into his hands, and he asked who had sent it to her, a merry rashness misled her into the jest of answering "Fabricius." She felt sure that Theophilus could not fail to see the joke. But, as she was unable to give her merry excited smile that shade of mockery at the mention of the absent one, which would have made the jest evident, Theophilus was firmly convinced that her sweet and genuine joy was due to the present and its giver, and that he had fallen into a nasty trap by intruding into a circle which was forbidden and strange to him. Confounded and ashamed, he cast down his eyes, began to tremble, and let the glittering ornament fall to the ground, where it was shivered to pieces.

In her first dismay, Dorothea forgot all about her joke, and almost forgot Theophilus, and could only stoop aghast to pick up the pieces, exclaiming "How clumsy!" without bestowing a look upon him; so that she did not see the alteration in his features, and had no suspicion that he had misunderstood her.

But, when she had risen, and, recovering herself quickly, turned towards him, Theophilus had already regained his proud self-command. He looked at her inscrutably and indifferently, begged almost mockingly for pardon, promising her full restitution for the vase which had come to grief, then bowed and left the garden.

Pale and sorrowful she looked after his slim figure, with the white toga wrapped closely about it, and his black curly head bent to one side as if his thoughts were already far away from her.

The waves of the silvery sea lapped soft and lazy against the marble steps on the beach, all else around was still, and Dorothea's little devices were at an end.

Weeping, she slipped away with the collected fragments of the vase to hide them in her room.

They did not see each other again for many months. Theophilus returned at once to the capital, and when Dorothea went back there in the autumn, he sedulously avoided encountering her; for the mere possibility of meeting her alarmed and excited him. So all their happiness was gone for the nonce.

The natural result was that she sought consolation in the new faith of her parents, and as soon as they observed this, they lost no time in deciding their child in her resolution, and initiating her fully into their faith and practice.

Meanwhile, Dorothea's assumed friendliness for the governor had also its unfortunate effect, in that Fabricius considered himself justified in renewing his courtship with redoubled energy. He was all the more surprised, therefore, when Dorothea could scarcely endure the sight of him, and he seemed to have become more repugnant to her than Misfortune herself. But he did not draw back on that account; rather, he increased his importunity and began to quarrel with her because of her new faith, and to assail her conscience as he mingled flatteries with thinly-veiled threats.

Dorothea, however, acknowledged her faith openly and fearlessly, and turned away from him as from an unsubstantial shadow which cannot be seen.

Theophilus heard of all this, and how the good maiden was not having the happiest life of it. What surprised him most was the news that she would have nothing whatever to do with the proconsul. Although he was old-world or indifferent in the matter of religion, he was not offended at the maiden's new faith, and with his partiality for her he began to be more in her company again, the better to see and hear how she was faring. But in her present mood, she could speak of nothing except in the tenderest and most languishing accents of a Heavenly Bridegroom whom she had found, who was awaiting her in immortal beauty, to take her to His radiant breast, and give her the rose of eternal life, and so forth.

He could make neither head nor tail of this language. It offended and annoyed him, and filled his heart with a strange, painful jealousy of the unknown God who perverted a weak woman's mind; for he could not understand and interpret the excited and enthusiastic Dorothea's expressions otherwise than in the old mythological fashion. Jealousy of a superhuman being did not hurt his pride, but it blunted his sympathy with the woman who boasted of being united to deities. Yet it was nothing else than her unrequited love for himself that put such language into her mouth, just as he himself had the thorn of passion always fixed in his heart.

Matters had dragged on thus for some little time, when Fabricius suddenly pounced down. Taking advantage of renewed Imperial orders for a persecution of Christians, he had Dorothea and her parents imprisoned. The daughter, however, was placed in a separate gaol, and put to the question about her faith. Full of curiosity, he went in person and heard her loudly repudiating the ancient gods, and confessing as the only Lord of the world Christ, whose betrothed bride she was. At that, a savage jealousy took possession of the governor also. He resolved on her destruction, and ordered her to be tortured and, if she still persisted, to be put to death. Then he departed. She was laid on a gridiron, under which coals were fanned to a glow in such a fashion that the heat only increased slowly. Still, it hurt her tender frame. She uttered stifled screams for a time,

56

while her limbs, which were chained down to the gridiron, quivered, and tears flowed from her eyes. Theophilus, who usually refrained from taking any part in such persecutions, had heard of the business, and hastened to her full of horror and disquiet. Forgetful of his own safety, he thrust his way through the gaping populace, and, when with his own ears he heard Dorothea's low moans, he snatched a sword from a soldier's hand, and stood at one bound before her bed of torture.

"Does it hurt, Dorothea?" he enquired with a bitter smile, intending to cut her fastenings. But she answered, feeling suddenly as if all pain had left her and she were filled with the most perfect bliss, "How could it hurt me, Theophilus? It is the roses of my well-beloved Bridegroom that I am lying upon. See! To-day is my wedding-day!"

Her lips played as if it were one of her favourite dainty jests, while her eyes looked at him blissfully. An unearthly radiance seemed to illumine her and her couch, a triumphant calm settled upon her. Theophilus lowered his sword, threw it from him, and once again retreated ashamed and confounded as on that morning in the garden by the sea.

Then the coals glowed red again. Dorothea sighed and longed for death. And her desire was granted; she was led away to the place of execution, to be beheaded.

She went to her fate with a light step, followed by the unthinking, shouting mob. Standing by the roadside she saw Theophilus, who never took his eyes off her. Their eyes met. Dorothea stood still an instant, and said cheerfully, "Theophilus, if you only knew how beautiful and splendid are my Lord's rose-gardens, where I shall soon be walking, and how sweet his apples taste which grow there, you would come along with me!"

Theophilus responded with a bitter smile: "I'll tell you what, Dorothea! Send me some of your roses and apples for a sample when you get there!"

She gave a friendly nod, and went on her way.

Theophilus followed her with his eyes until the cloud of dust, golden in the evening sunshine, which accompanied the procession, had vanished in the distance, and the street was empty and silent. Then with shrouded head he went home, and ascended with faltering steps to the house-top, from which there was a view out to the Argeus mountains. The place of execution was situated on one of the foot-hills. He could easily make out a dark cluster of humanity there, and he stretched out his longing arms in its direction. He fancied that in the light of the departing sun he could see the flash of the falling axe, and he dropped down and lay prone on the terrace. And, as a matter of fact, Dorothea's head did fall about that time.

But he had not long lain thus motionless, when a clear shining lightened the twilight, and pierced with blinding radiance beneath Theophilus's hands in which his face lay buried, and poured itself into his closed eyes like liquid gold. At the same time a rare fragrance filled the air. The young man arose as if pervaded by some new and unknown life. Before him stood a wondrous lovely boy, with golden ringlets, clad in a star-spangled garment, and with radiant naked feet, bearing a small basket in no less radiant hands. The basket was filled with the most beautiful roses, the like of which were never seen, and among the roses lay three apples of Paradise.

With an infinitely true-hearted and frank childish smile, yet not without a certain pleasant roguishness, the child said, "This is from Dorothea!" put the basket in his hands with the question, "Have you got it?" and vanished.

The basket did not vanish, and Theophilus had really got it in his hands. He found the three apples lightly marked by two tiny teeth, as was the custom among lovers in ancient times. He ate them slowly, with the blazing starry heavens above him. A mighty longing permeated him with a sweet fire, and, clasping the basket to his breast and concealing it with his mantle, he hastened down from the house-top, through the streets and into the palace of the governor, who was sitting at table endeavouring to drown his wild rage in untempered Colchian wine.

With flashing eyes, Theophilus advanced towards him, without uncovering the basket, and exclaimed before the whole company, "I declare that I am of the same faith as Dorothea, whom you have just now murdered. It is the only true faith!"

"Then go after the witch!" retorted the governor, who, racked by sudden wrath and consuming jealousy, sprang to his feet, and had his secretary beheaded that same hour.

Thus Theophilus was, after all, united for ever to Dorothea on that same day. She welcomed him with the restful look of the blessed. Like two doves, separated by the tempest, who have found each other again, and first fly in a wide circuit round their home, so the united pair swept hand in hand swiftly, swiftly, and unceasingly around the outmost circles of Heaven, freed from every weight, yet still themselves. Then they separated sportively and lost themselves in wide infinity, while each knew where the other tarried, and what the other thought, and joined with him in embracing every creature and all existence in sweet love. Then they sought each other again with waxing desire, which knew no pain and no impatience. They found each other, and once more eddied about, or reposed in contemplation of themselves and gazed near and far into the world of infinitude. But once in blissful forgetfulness they ventured too near the crystal habitation of the Holy Trinity, and entered within. There they lost all consciousness, and like twins beneath a mother's heart they fell on sleep, and no doubt are sleeping still, unless meantime they have been able to make their way out.

A LEGEND OF THE DANCE

O virgin of Israel: thou shalt again be adorned with thy tabrets, and shalt go forth in the dances.... Then shall the virgin rejoice in the dance, both young men and old together.

Jeremiah, xxxi. 4, 13.

According to Saint Gregory, Musa was the dancer among the saints. The child of good people, she was a bright young lady, a diligent servant of the Mother of God, and subject only to one weakness, such an uncontrollable passion for the dance, that when the child was not praying she was dancing without fail, and that on all imaginable occasions. Musa danced with her playmates, with children, with the young men, and even by herself. She danced in her own room and every other room in the house, in the garden, in the meadows. Even when she went to the altar, it was to a gracious measure rather than at a walk, and even on the smooth marble flags before the church-door she did not scruple to practise a few hasty steps.

In fact, one day when she found herself alone in the church, she could not refrain from executing some figures before the altar, and, so to speak, dancing a pretty prayer to the Virgin Mary. She became so oblivious of all else that she fancied she was merely dreaming when she saw an oldish but handsome gentleman dancing opposite her, and supplementing her figures so skilfully that the pair got into the most elaborate dance imaginable. The gentleman had a royal purple robe, a golden crown on his head, and a glossy black curled beard, which the silvery streaks of age had touched as with distant starlight. At the same time music sounded from the choir, where half-a-dozen small angels stood or sat with their chubby little legs hanging over the screen, and fingered or blew their various instruments. The urchins were very pleasant and skilful. Each rested his music on one of the stone angels with which the choir-screen was adorned, except the smallest, a puffy-cheeked piper, who sat cross-legged, and contrived to hold his music with his pink toes. He was the most diligent of them all. The others dangled their feet, kept spreading their pinions, one or other of them, with a rustle, so that their colours shimmered like doves' breasts, and they teased each other as they played.

Musa found no time to wonder at all this until the dance, which lasted a pretty long time, was over; for the merry gentleman seemed to enjoy himself as much as the maid, who felt as if she were dancing about in Heaven. But when the music ceased, and Musa stood there panting, she began to be scared in good earnest, and looked in astonishment at the ancient, who was neither out of breath nor warm, and who now began to speak. He introduced himself as David, the Virgin Mary's royal ancestor and her ambassador. And he asked if she would like to pass eternal bliss in an unending pleasure-dance, compared with which the dance they had just finished could only be called a miserable crawl.

To this she promptly answered that there was nothing she desired better. Whereupon the blessed King David said again that in that case she had nothing more to do than to renounce all pleasure and all dancing for the rest of her days on earth, and devote herself wholly to penance and spiritual exercises, and that without hesitation or relapse.

The maiden was taken aback at these conditions, and she asked whether she must really give up dancing altogether. She questioned, indeed, whether there was any dancing in Heaven; for there was a time for everything: this earth looked very fit and proper for dancing; it stood to reason that Heaven must have very different attractions, else death were a superfluity.

But David explained to her that her notions on this subject were quite erroneous, and proved from many Bible texts, and from his own example, that dancing was most assuredly a sanctified occupation for the blessed. But what was wanted just now was an immediate decision, Yes or No, whether she wished to enter into eternal joy by way of temporal self-denial or not. If she did not, then he would go farther on; for they wanted some dancers in Heaven.

Musa stood, still doubtful and undecided, and fumbled anxiously with her finger-tips in her mouth. It seemed too hard never to dance again from that moment, all for the sake of an unknown reward.

At that David gave a signal, and suddenly the musicians struck up some bars of a dance of such unheard-of bliss and unearthliness that the girl's soul leapt in her body, and all her limbs twitched; but she could not get one of them to dance, and she noted that her body was far too heavy and stiff for that tune. Full of longing she struck her hand into the king's, and made the promise which he demanded.

Forthwith he was no more to be seen, and the angel-musicians whirred and fluttered, and crowded out and away through an open window; but, in mischievous, childish fashion, before going, they dealt the patient stone angels a sounding slap on the cheeks with their rolled-up music.

Musa went home with devout step, carrying that celestial melody in her ears; and, having laid all her dainty raiment aside, she got a coarse gown made and put it on. At the same time, she built herself a cell at the bottom of her parents' garden, where the deep shade of the trees lingered, made a scant bed of moss, and from that day onwards separated herself from all her kindred, and took up her abode there as a penitent and saint. She spent all her time in prayer, and often disciplined herself with a scourge. But her severest penance consisted in holding her limbs stiff and immovable; for whenever she heard a sound, the twitter of a bird, or the rustling of the leaves in the wind, her feet twitched, as much as to tell her they must dance.

As this involuntary twitching would not forsake her, and often seduced her to a little skip before she was aware, she caused her tender little feet to be fastened together by a light chain. Her relatives and friends marvelled day and night at the transformation, rejoiced to possess such a saint, and guarded the hermitage under the trees as the apple of their eye. Many came for her counsel and intercession. In particular, they used to bring young girls to her who were rather clumsy on their feet; for it was observed that every one whom she touched at once became light and graceful in gait.

So she spent three years in her cell; but, by the end of the third year, Musa had become almost as thin and transparent as a summer cloud. She lay continually on her bed of moss, gazed wistfully into Heaven, and was convinced that she could already see the golden sandals of the blessed, dancing and gliding about through the azure.

At last, one harsh autumn day, the tidings spread that the saint lay on her death-bed. She had taken off her dark penitential robe, and caused herself to be arrayed in bridal garments of dazzling white. So she lay with folded hands, and smilingly awaited the hour of death. The garden was all filled with devout persons, the breezes murmured, and the leaves were falling from the trees on all sides. But suddenly the sighing of the wind changed into music, which appeared to be playing in the tree-tops, and, as the people looked up, lo! all the branches were clad in fresh green, the myrtles and pomegranates put out blossom and fragrance, the earth decked itself with flowers, and a rosy glow settled upon the white, frail form of the dying saint.

That same instant, she yielded up her spirit. The chain about her feet sprang asunder with a sharp twang, Heaven opened wide all around, full of unbounded radiance, so that all could see in. Then they saw many thousands of beautiful young men and maidens in the utmost splendour, dancing circle upon circle farther than the eye could reach. A magnificent king, throned on a cloud with a special band of six small angels seated on its edge, bore down a little way towards earth, and received the form of the sainted Musa from before the eyes of all the beholders who filled the garden. They saw, too, how she sprang into the opened Heaven, and immediately danced out of sight among the jubilant, radiant circles.

That was a high feast-day in Heaven. Now the custom--to be sure, it is denied by Saint Gregory of Nyssa; but it is stoutly maintained by his namesake of Nazianza--the custom on feast-days was to invite the Nine Muses, who sat for the rest of their time in Hell, and to admit them to Heaven, that they might be of assistance. They were well entertained; but, once the feast was over, had to go back to the other place.

When now the dances and songs and all the ceremonies had come to an end, and the Heavenly company sat down, Musa was taken to a table where the Nine Muses were being served. They sat huddled together half-scared, glancing about them with their fiery black or dark-blue eyes. The busy Martha of the gospels was caring for them in person; she had on her finest kitchen-apron and a tiny little smut on her white chin, and was pressing all manner of good things on the Muses in the friendliest possible way. But when Musa and Saint Cæcilia and some other artistic women arrived, and greeted the shy Pierians cheerfully and joined their company, they began to thaw, grew confidential, and the feminine circle became quite pleasant and happy. Musa sat beside Terpsiehore, and Cæcilia between Polyhymnia and Euterpe, and all took one another's hands. Next came the little minstrel urchins, and made up to the pretty women, with an eye to the bright fruit which shone on the ambrosial table. King David himself came and brought a golden cup, out of which all drank, so that gracious joy warmed them. He went round the table in high good-spirits, not omitting, as he passed, to chuck pretty Erato under the chin. While things were going on so famously at the Muses' table, our Gracious Lady herself appeared in all her beauty and goodness, sat down a few minutes beside the Muses, and kissed the august Urania with the starry coronet tenderly upon the lips, when she took her departure, whispering to her that she would not rest until the Muses could remain in Paradise for ever.

But that never came about. To declare their gratitude for the kindness and friendliness which had been shown them, and to prove their good will, the Muses took counsel together and practised a hymn of praise in a retired corner of the under-world. They tried to give it the form of the solemn chorals which were the fashion in Heaven. They arranged it in two parts of four voices each, with a sort of principal part which Urania took, and they thus produced a remarkable piece of vocal music.

The next time that a feast-day was celebrated in Heaven, and the Muses again rendered their assistance, they seized what appeared to be a favourable moment for their purpose, took their places, and commenced their song. It began softly, but soon swelled out mightily. But in those regions it sounded so dismal, almost defiant and harsh, yet so wistful and mournful, that first of all a horrified silence prevailed, and next the whole assembly was seized with a sad longing for earth and home, and broke into universal weeping.

A sigh without end throbbed through Heaven. All the Elders and Prophets hastened up in dismay, while the Muses, with the best of intentions, sang louder and more mournfully, and all Paradise with the Patriarchs and Elders and Prophets, and all who ever walked or lay in the green pastures, lost all command of themselves. Until at last, the High and Mighty Trinity Himself came to put things right, and reduced the too-zealous Muses to silence with a long, reverberating peal of thunder.

Then quiet and composure were restored to Heaven. But the poor Nine Sisters had to depart, and never dared enter it again from that day.

THE END

Made in the USA
San Bernardino, CA
31 January 2017